MW00398312

Thank you to all my readers who followed this story as I wrote it serially, and especially to those who gave me feedback along the way, making this book so much fun to write.

ONE

I'm not the kind of girl that bad boys want to screw.

I'm the kind of girl that nice guys want to take home to meet their overprotective Catholic mamas.

This was a fact of my existence that was never going to change. I'd reconciled myself to it a long time ago.

In high school and college, none of the athletes or cool rebel types looked at me twice. It was the quiet, nerdy guys who would work their courage up and ask me out to dances or the movies. My social life improved when I started law school, but it was still only the nice ones that would show me any interest.

I'm sure men never processed it consciously, but they'd take one look at my smooth, shiny hair and my clear, pale skin and my childbearing hips, and something would click in their brains. They could introduce me to their parents, but they wouldn't proposition me for a one-night stand.

I wasn't hot-fling material.

All this is to explain why it was so bizarre and unusual for me to be getting off an elevator in an expensive hotel and walking toward a corner room.

For sex.

I was here for *sex*.

I'd never done anything like it before.

I glanced in an ornate mirror halfway down the hall and paused, momentarily feeling like Jamie Lee Curtis in that old movie that still gets played on cable channels where she's married to a spy and realizes she needs to sexify herself before entering a hotel room. I'd come here straight from work. All the women in my law firm wore stylish pantsuits in subdued colors, so that was what I wore too. I had a closet full of them. Mine was charcoal gray today, and I'd paired it with a pale lavender top. I'd spent a whole month's paycheck on my designer heels, but they were barely visible under the hem of my trousers. I looked fine, appropriate for the hotel and almost any professional occasion.

I didn't look sexy though.

Sean Doyle wasn't waiting in that room to take me home to meet his mother. He was waiting to take me to bed.

I tried to tousle my hair like Jamie Lee Curtis, but my hair was long and straight and strawberry blond, and it simply would not tousle. I couldn't unbutton my top more—since there weren't any buttons—and my neckline was too high to get any sort of cleavage action. I started to take off my jacket so at least my arms would be bare, but I decided against it.

This was me. Pretty in a boring, good-girl way. Always on time for appointments and never causing a scene.

Vanilla all the way through.

Even so, Sean had wanted to fuck me last week. He'd had me against a wall in the back hallway of a bar, dry humping me, his tongue in my mouth. We'd both had way too much to drink that night, but he'd wanted me for real. If someone hadn't come back to use the restroom, we probably would have gone all the way, right there against the wall.

He'd wanted me then, and he'd asked me to meet him here tonight—well, he'd discreetly handed me a business card at yesterday's meeting with the place and time scrawled on the back—so he must still want me tonight.

Sean might not be the man from my romantic daydreams. That man had a very clear face, and that face would never be Sean's. But it didn't matter.

I was here now, and I was going to do this. I moved away from the mirror, walked the rest of the way down the hall to room 1212, and I knocked on the door before I chickened out.

The door swung open after about thirty seconds, and Sean Doyle stood in front of me.

He was wearing a suit too—a much more expensive suit than mine. He had a Damien Lewis thing going for him (without the red hair). He was intensely attractive in a way you couldn't really figure out. His features weren't traditionally handsome, but his eyes were deep green, heavy-lidded, and intelligent, and his mouth was interesting, mobile, and undeniably sexy. His hair was brown, and he didn't always shave.

He arched his eyebrows with a little quirk of a smile. "Hi, Ash. I wasn't sure you'd come."

My name is Ashley, and no one calls me anything else. But he'd called me Ash last week at the bar as well. I wasn't sure if he had my name wrong or if he'd shortened it on purpose, but I didn't correct him. I liked how the name sounded in his slightly husky voice. "I wasn't sure myself." When he just stood there looking at me, I felt self-conscious, so I added tartly, "Am I allowed in?"

"Oh. Yeah. Of course." He stepped aside to let me into the big, fancy room.

The only details I noticed were the lovely king-size bed and the huge windows looking out onto downtown Boston.

"Do you want some wine?" he asked after we both stood for a minute in silence.

"Yes. Please." Last Thursday I'd had several drinks before I'd made a move on him. Maybe a couple of glasses of wine would help tonight.

There was a bottle of expensive merlot on the table near the window with two glasses. Sean went to pour it out. When I saw a file folder next to the wine, I went over to see what it was.

I was about to open the folder when Sean's hand closed down on it. His fingers were long and strong and slender, and his fingernails were clean and trimmed but not perfect. He obviously didn't get manicures. I wasn't sure why I noticed it, but I did.

"What is that?" I demanded, lifting my eyes from the file folder to his face.

"That's for after."

"After what?"

His eyebrows arched again, and his green eyes took on that hot look I remembered from last Thursday.

I felt my cheeks flushing. I knew exactly what he wanted to happen before we looked in that file folder.

Despite the complete lack of seduction or romance between us, I felt a little clench between my legs. Sean might not be the man I loved, but there was something so tangible and intense about him—like there was an energy radiating from his lean body that I could feel down to my core.

That I wanted to feel even more.

But I was curious now, so I waited until Sean lifted his hand to pick up his wineglass.

Then I reached over and snatched up the file folder.

"Hey!" he objected, trying to grab it from me.

I'd already taken three steps away and was starting to read the papers inside the file.

It was a contract.

A *contract*.

I stared down at the top sheet, my eyes wide with amazement.

"I told you that was for after." He slanted an almost sheepish look at me and glanced away when I met his eyes.

"You want me to sign a contract for our one-night stand?" I asked when I could finally speak.

"If it's a one-night stand, no. If you want it to continue, then yes. That's why I said it was for after."

I stared at him for a minute. Then I stared at the contract. Then I stared back at him.

He had the grace to look slightly embarrassed, but there was an ironic amusement glinting at the back of his eyes.

"I do what my lawyer tells me," he added. "You're a lawyer. You know what they're like."

I couldn't help it. I burst into laughter.

Sean narrowed his eyes. "You don't have to sign it. It's just if you—"

"Want it to continue," I finished for him, still giggling a little. I was scanning the pages of the contract one by one. "So if I want more than this one night, we'd meet here every other Wednesday night. No contact of any kind between our evenings together—no calls, texts, emails, meetings, nothing. We can't tell anyone else about us. And we can end it at any point without explanation." I paused, looking up from the pages. "If we don't keep in touch between Wednesday nights, what happens if we can't make it one Wednesday but we don't want to call the whole thing off?"

Sean stepped over so he was beside me. He reached over to flip a page and point to a clause halfway down the page. "We leave a message at the front desk of the hotel." He studied my face with narrowed eyes. "I know it probably sounds ridiculous to you, but I have to be careful."

I believed him. I was just a normal person. I'd never even imagine signing contracts for sex. Sean, however, was incredibly rich, incredibly successful, and incredibly well known—at least in the Boston area. A local boy made good. Instead of becoming a cop like the rest of his family, he'd gone to college and then gotten an MBA and started a real estate development business that had taken off beyond all expectations. If the news got out that he was dating—or even meeting some random woman for sex—it would be hot gossip all over town. I could understand why he'd want to avoid that, especially for a relationship that was obviously intended to be no strings attached.

I was still trying to suppress a smile. "How many times have you signed this particular contract?"

His fiancée had died two years ago, so he could have had any number of contracted liaisons since then.

He flipped another page and pointed toward a paragraph I hadn't yet read.

I giggled. "No personal questions about our sexual pasts. Got it."

When I looked back up at him, I realized something else, something new.

He might realize how crazy it seemed to someone else, but he was serious about the contract. And it wasn't just to protect him from stalkers and the gossip columns.

It was to protect him emotionally.

He'd loved a woman once, and he'd lost her. He was the only man I'd ever met who had a tragic origin story like Batman. No one knew who had done it—if it was a targeted hit or a mugging gone wrong—but both he and his fiancée had been shot walking home from a play two years ago. She'd been killed, and he'd been in the hospital for almost a month. The story had been front-page news for weeks, so I knew all about him, even though I'd only met him for the first time last month when I was part of the legal team representing the other party in a huge property deal he was working on.

I'd only finished law school four years ago. I'd been the junior member of the team from my firm, and so I hadn't said a word to him. I hadn't even realized he'd noticed me at all until he came up to me at the bar last week and offered to buy me a second drink.

Sean was thirty-eight—ten years older than me. His heart might have been forever crushed when his fiancée died, but he was still a healthy, virile man, and he would want to keep having sex.

So this contract allowed him to have sex without any emotional complications, without ever putting his heart at risk.

I'd been correct from the beginning—when I'd first seen him across the conference room in his fancy downtown offices. He was completely unavailable to me, and he always would be. His body was all he was offering.

It was fine. My body was all I had to offer too.

After all, I was in love with someone else.

I closed the file folder. "Okay. I wouldn't be opposed to signing this, assuming the sex is good enough for us to want to do it again."

Sean's expression changed, became hot. His eyebrows arched again in that slightly smug way. "You really doubt it's going to be good?"

I gave him a playful little shrug. "Well, all you've done so far is give me a glass of wine and review a contract, so I'm not sure why I'm supposed to believe you're some sort of sex god or—"

I couldn't finish my sentence because Sean had grabbed me and pulled me into a hard kiss.

The sudden move was startling, so I was motionless for a moment, letting him kiss me.

I don't know if you've ever kissed a stranger, but it's weird. *Very* weird. Without alcohol to cloud your brain, it feels almost unnatural, like your body is doing something that doesn't match your reality.

That was how it felt then. I'd only had a few sips of wine. It wasn't nearly enough to throw off inhibitions. Sean was a good kisser. His mouth was skillful, agile, and his body was warm and hard against mine. He must have brushed his teeth after work like I had since he tasted slightly of toothpaste. And he smelled good—really good—a faint mingling of natural and expensive, which was exactly what I liked.

But still. It was so incredibly strange to be kissing him in this hotel room at six forty-five on a Wednesday evening.

He pulled back after a minute, his eyes searching my face. "No?" he asked softly.

I was nervous and uncomfortable and a little dizzy, so I did what I always did. I covered it with tartness. "Not no. But I'm not half-drunk today. You're going to have to try a little harder."

His mouth made that sexy little twist of amusement, and he pulled me toward him again. This time he went a little slower, his tongue tracing the line of my lips as his hand stroked down my hair to my back and then even lower.

It felt good. I started to respond. My tongue slid out to meet his, and I reached out to feel his firm back, his thick hair. And before I knew it, we were walking over toward the bed, still tangled in an embrace.

I started to pull off my jacket as he kept kissing me. I couldn't help but be a little thrilled that he didn't seem to want to let go of me. His body was getting tenser by the second, so I figured he must be getting turned on.

8

When I got stuck in the sleeves of my jacket, he helped me pull it off. Then he tugged off my top, his eyes moving with a hot urgency over my bare skin and pretty bra.

I'd worn my best underwear set—lavender satin and lace—and Sean seemed to like what he saw as he stared at me.

When I began to feel self-conscious, I leaned over to slide off my shoes and then my trousers.

"Fuck, you're gorgeous," he breathed. Sean reached over like he was going to take off my bra, but I distracted him by grabbing the lapels of his jacket and working it off over his shoulders.

I wasn't going to be completely naked while he had all his clothes on. No way that was going to happen.

We got rid of his jacket, tie, shirt, belt and shoes, and then he seemed to get impatient all of a sudden. He sank into another kiss, and it was so enthusiastic that we ended up tumbling onto the bed.

He rolled us over so he was on top of me and gave me a little smile. "What do you like?" His green eyes were still raking over my face and body. I was always trying to lose the same ten pounds, and I'd never gotten a tan in my life. My skin was pale and smooth and tight, and my breasts were full and rounded, but I'd never been comfortable showing off my body. Even in bed. Even with men who weren't strangers.

"What do you mean, what do I like?"

"I mean, what works for you?" He raised his eyes to meet mine.

"Normal things."

"What does that mean?"

"It means I like normal things. What do you think it means? I'm not into chains and whips, if that's what you're wondering."

He chuckled, and the sound shook his body deliciously. "That's not what I was asking. I'm trying to be a nice guy here and find out what works for you."

I'd been with four other men in my life—all of them relationships that had lasted at least six months—and no man had ever come right out and demanded I tell them what I liked in bed.

I had absolutely no idea what to say.

"I like foreplay," I finally responded, trying to sound confident, which I wasn't at all feeling. "But nothing too weird."

His eyes glinted as he lowered his head toward mine again. "Foreplay it is. And nothing weird."

I almost laughed. I really did. But then he was kissing me again and I forgot about laughing. He kissed me for a long time before he started to trail kisses down my neck. He teased me over my bra for a while until I was tense and gasping. When his face moved down to my belly, my whole body clenched.

"And I don't really like a guy's head between my legs until I know him better," I said, panting slightly.

He glanced up at my face and gave me a small nod as if he understood.

He was probably relieved. I mean, surely he hadn't been too excited about going down on me, although it was nice he'd been willing.

Raising his body again, he reached around to take off my bra. I could see the reaction in his face and body when he looked at my bare breasts. It was like something inside him had jumped in excitement.

He was hard in his trousers now. His whole body was tight. But he'd been serious about doing what I liked first, and he hadn't yet made a move to take off his pants.

We kissed again, and I could feel desire clenching between my legs. I still felt kind of self-conscious and uncomfortable though, and I was a little afraid I wasn't going to be able to come, even with Sean's purposeful attention.

"You could say something, you know." I wasn't sure why I'd spoken. Just that I needed to break the tension I was feeling.

He lifted his head to meet my eyes. "Dirty talk?"

I giggled. "Not really. I just meant we can talk. Unless you're not a talker."

"I think you know I'm a talker."

He was. He was incredibly smart and incredibly verbal. That much had been clear from the meetings I'd attended in his offices over the past few weeks. He wasn't the strong, silent type—despite his tragic history. He was charming and clever and articulate, and that was one of the things I liked about him.

"So talk," I said.

He frowned. "Now you've put me on the spot."

I laughed again, almost forgetting that I was lying beneath him wearing nothing but my panties.

He gazed down at me, his expression softening as if he liked what he saw on my face. "I noticed you the first time I saw you," he murmured.

"You did not. You were in full business mode. You barely knew I existed."

He'd started kissing my neck, teasing and nibbling in a way that made me shiver, but he replied against my skin, "I knew you existed. I saw you there, sitting so quietly, trying to fade into the background like you were afraid someone would notice you and realize you weren't supposed to be there."

That was exactly how I'd felt in the first couple of meetings. It was a real coup that I'd been asked to work on the team—it was the first big job I'd been given since joining the firm three years ago—and I'd been terrified I was going to blow it.

He'd moved down to my breasts now, nuzzling slightly before he teased one nipple with his tongue.

I gasped as the jolt of pleasure took me by surprise because I'd been distracted by the conversation.

"I wasn't that bad," I managed to say, shifting beneath him to ease the tightening pressure of arousal. "I acted just like everyone else."

"I know you did. But I still noticed you. All that red hair and sexy lips and that gorgeous body you were trying to hide with those boring suits. I knew you had a fire inside you that you'd never let out before."

"That's…" I couldn't finish the sentence because he was suckling my nipple in a way that made me want to moan. I closed my eyes and tossed my head and managed to try again. "That's presumptuous. I'll have you know I've always had a great sex life."

It wasn't entirely true, but it was partially true. I'd had good sex before, and there was no reason for him to assume I hadn't.

"I believe you. That's not what I meant."

I wanted to know what he meant, if it wasn't that he didn't think I'd had hot sex before, but he didn't explain himself further. His hands had moved down to part my legs, and his fingers slipped beneath my underwear until he was touching me intimately.

He would feel how hot and wet I was. He couldn't help but feel it.

I groaned helplessly as he stroked me there and kept teasing my nipple with his tongue. The pleasure tugged between the two parts of my body until I couldn't tell where it was coming from.

"I saw you sitting there every day, and every day I wondered what was going on in your mind. And what your body would feel like in bed with me."

Two of his fingers were inside me now, and I felt myself clenching down around the penetration.

"There it is," he murmured thickly, lifting his head as if he wanted to see my face. "Is it the talk or the foreplay that's working for you?"

"I don't know," I gasped, rocking my hips against his fingers. The pleasure had taken form now, momentum, and I needed it to get where it was going. "Just don't stop."

He kept pumping his fingers and lowered his face to my other breast. He sucked on the nipple, making me writhe and clench my fingers into the bedding beneath me.

"I saw you go into the bar last Thursday," he murmured, releasing my breast for long enough to talk. "And so I went in after you."

"You did?" My voice squeaked just a little.

"Of course. You didn't think my finding you there was an accident, did you?" He flicked my tight nipple with his tongue until I let out a shameless moan. Then he added, "I wasn't following you or anything. I just happened to see you go into the bar. And I wanted to see what you were really like beneath the surface."

"And now you know," I gasped. I was so close to coming I could feel it. I was chasing it with my hips, my whole body.

"Now I know." He gave my nipple one hard little nip.

I came apart at the sudden jolt of pain, the orgasm clamping down and then releasing in waves of pleasure. I made a loud embarrassing sound that was half groan and half sob as my body shook and tried to ride his fingers until the spasms finally faded.

He was smiling when I finally opened my eyes, as if he were very pleased with himself.

For no good reason his expression embarrassed me. It made me feel strangely young and inexperienced.

So my tone was tarter than it should have been as I said, "You don't have to look quite so proud of yourself. It wasn't *that* good."

His smile widened. "Yes, it was. And I bet that jackass you're in love with wouldn't take the time to get you off first the way I did."

I gasped, this time in indignation. "Yes, he would! And he's not a jackass!"

"Yes, he is."

"You don't even know him."

"I know everything I need to know about him. I sized him up in about a minute when he first walked into my conference room. I've known plenty of guys like him before."

That's the other thing to know about me. The man I was in love with was also a lawyer in my firm. He also specialized in property law. I saw him in the hall and in the break room every day, and he was always nice to me in a light, playful way. He'd led the team that had been negotiating the contract with Sean over the past month.

If I hadn't gotten drunk last week, I never would have admitted to Sean—to anyone—that I'd been in love with John Cooper from the first time I'd laid eyes on him, from my very first day at work in the firm. It was true, but it wasn't something I ever told anyone.

He wasn't in love with me. He'd never even tried to get to know me outside the context of work. It was one of those hopeless unrequited loves that eat away at you and never come to fruition, and I knew it.

If I hadn't known it, I never would have ended up in bed with Sean Doyle.

"Admit it," Sean said, still smiling in that smugly pleased way. "Your jackass would have been in and out in about five minutes, and you'd have had to finish yourself off after he left."

I scowled at him. "That's not true at all. You don't know him. Now shut up and take your pants off."

He was chuckling low in his throat as he did as I said, and I couldn't help but watch with interest as he bared himself. His body was strong and lean and natural—he wasn't unusually hairy, but he obviously didn't believe in manscaping—and his erection was thick and heavy.

I really liked the looks of him, and I liked how *real* he seemed.

He wasn't the love of my life—stepping out of my daydreams or a sexy fantasy. He was a real, human man, slanting me a look of ironic inquiry.

And now he was sliding off my panties, reaching over for a condom, and then positioning himself between my legs.

I still couldn't believe I was doing this.

We didn't talk as he rolled on the condom and then lined himself up at my entrance. I was still very wet, very aroused, so there wouldn't be any worry about discomfort. He held himself up on one arm, and I bent my knees, and then he was starting to push himself in.

I had another one of those moments of strangeness—that this guy I barely knew was putting his penis inside me—

but it didn't feel bad. It felt full and stretched and intense. Sean let out a low groan as he finished the thrust.

"How is it?" he asked hoarsely. He'd turned his head slightly, and his eyes were focused on the pillow on the other side of the bed.

"Fine. Good. It's good." I rolled my hips, trying to relax my muscles even more.

Sean groaned again. His jaw must have been clenched because I saw a muscle flickering on the side of his face.

When he just held himself still, I finally asked, "So are you going to move or what?"

He turned his head back to meet my eyes. "Kind of impatient, aren't you?"

"I don't think so. When a guy is inside me, I expect him to do something. Unless you're thinking I'm going to do all the work."

He gave a huff of amusement, and then he seemed to lose control for a minute, making a few fast, short pushes into me.

It felt so good I gasped and arched up.

After that, we didn't talk anymore. His focus had narrowed down to a hot, urgent motion, and that was clearly the only thing filling his mind. He held on to one of my legs, pushing my knee toward my chest and spreading me open for him. He moved in fast, steady thrusts, his eyes moving hungrily from my face to my breasts to where he was pumping into me.

The look on his face, as much as his motion inside me, was causing pleasure to tighten again at my center.

I occasionally came during intercourse, but it wasn't a regular thing. So I was surprised when I felt another orgasm rising up inside me.

"Fuck," he muttered. "Fuck, you feel so good."

No girl didn't want to hear that, especially when he obviously meant it. He was totally into this, all his attention and energy channeled into the way he was fucking me right now.

Sean's thrusting was getting harder and faster as he was starting to lose control. "Fuck. You're getting tighter. Oh fuck!"

I was panting just as much as he was now, and my fingers were digging into the back of his neck. He'd pushed my knee back even farther until it almost met my shoulder. The bed was rocking shamelessly, and in another situation, I would have been embarrassed, afraid the people in the next room would be able to hear how hard he was taking me. But I didn't even care. I wanted it, wanted even more of it.

"Fuck, Ash," he gasped, his face twisting dramatically, clearly right on the cusp of coming. "How do you feel this good?"

It was his words as much as the stimulation that pushed me over the edge again. I gave a soft, breathless sob as I shook helplessly through an orgasm.

He wasn't holding back anymore. He was pushing into me hard, with a clumsy kind of roughness. It didn't hurt. It just felt raw and urgent and nakedly real, like he wasn't putting on any kind of show—and neither was I.

When he came, I could see the rush of pleasure on his face, and he let out a loud, uncontrolled sound.

We were both breathless as we came down, sweating and gasping and limp. It took him a minute to catch his breath before he pulled out of me and rolled over, his eyes closed and still holding on to the condom.

I felt sore and tingling between my legs, and I was suddenly a little embarrassed again. So I said, "I'll take care of that if you want."

He opened his eyes and looked a bit surprised, but he tied off the condom, and let me take it.

I threw it away in the bathroom and then washed my hands. I stared at myself in the mirror, flushed cheeks, wild look in my blue eyes.

I couldn't believe I'd just done that.

I'd had sex with Sean Doyle—a man I barely knew—and it had been odd but still really good.

I wouldn't mind doing it again.

I decided to use the bathroom since I was in here, so I peed and then I cleaned myself up a bit. Feeling better, I grabbed a bathrobe from a hook and put it on as I returned to the bed.

Now that sex was over, I didn't want him peering at my body.

He was still lying on top of the sheets, completely naked, his eyes closed. He looked relaxed, sated—and it made me just a little bit proud.

He'd had a really good time. With me. And now he was satisfied.

I went to get my glass of wine from the table.

"Grab mine too, if you don't mind," he said.

When I handed him his wine, he took my hand and pulled me back into the bed with him. I propped myself up on the pillows and smiled at him.

"So what do you think?" he asked.

"About what?"

He frowned. "You know what. Should we sign the contract or not?"

"I wouldn't be opposed to it." I didn't want to sound too excited, after all. I couldn't let him think that I was already looking forward to the Wednesday after next.

"Yeah?" His eyes were searching my face, as if trying to read my mind.

"Yeah. What about you?"

"I would have signed it even before we had sex," he admitted.

"What? You had no idea whether we'd even be good together or not."

"I was pretty sure we'd be good."

I shook my head at him, not sure whether he was telling the truth or just being cocky in that teasing way he had.

"And you'd really be okay with the… the limitations?" He was still looking for something in my face.

"Why wouldn't I be?"

"Well, this works out perfectly for me. I'm never going to fall in love again, and I'd rather not deal with the complications of dating since it will never lead anywhere. But you want to fall in love, so this can't be what you're really looking for. I don't want to take advantage of you."

I rolled my eyes. "That's patronizing. I can make informed decisions about my own sex life, and if I agree to it, it's not going to be because I'm secretly longing for you to fall for me."

His eyebrows shot up. "I never thought you were."

"Good. Because I'm in love with someone else, and right now I can't have him. Good sex is good sex, and it's better than nothing."

He chuckled wryly. "Very flattering. Thanks." Despite his words, he looked almost relieved.

And I realized something else then. Sean might be rich and powerful and accustomed to getting what he wanted, but at heart he was a really decent guy. He wanted a situation where he could have sex with absolutely no strings, but he didn't want to hurt me in the process.

I liked that about him.

And I knew I wasn't going to get hurt.

My heart belonged to someone else, so there was no danger of my ever giving it to Sean.

I finished my wine and set the glass on the bedside table. Then I got up and walked over to pick up the contract and the pen.

I scrawled my name on the signature line.

Sean was smiling as I brought it over to him. He signed it too.

"So I'll see you two weeks from tonight," I said.

"You're leaving already?" He was still completely naked, but he didn't look the least bit self-conscious about it.

"Yeah. I think so." I was feeling pretty good right now—like it had been a very good evening—but I was afraid if I stayed much longer, it would begin to get awkward.

I leaned over to pick up my clothes. "I had a good time though."

"Me too." His smile was real and companionable, but it was clearly not mushy or romantic.

He was never going to want anything but sex from me, and that was just fine with me. He was a good guy, and he was good in bed.

That was all I needed.

He wasn't my first choice for sex, and I obviously wasn't his. It didn't matter.

Second best was better than nothing.

TWO

So here's the scoop on John Cooper, the love of my life who didn't know it yet.

I met him for the first time on the day I started my job. I was getting coffee in the break area for my corner of offices and pretending to be poised and self-assured, as if I were completely comfortable in my new position and in my semi-expensive suit.

I wasn't. Of course I wasn't. I could barely believe I'd been given the job offer, and I was living with this lurking fear that someone would realize they'd made a mistake, that they'd actually wanted to hire another Ashley with red hair who'd graduated at the top of her class in a midtier law school and they'd mistakenly ended up with me instead.

Naturally, I didn't want anyone in the world to know I was feeling that way.

That first morning, I was using all my willpower to put on a confident demeanor as I poured a cup of coffee from the pot. When I turned around, mug in hand, the most handsome man I'd ever seen was standing less than a foot away.

He had very dark hair and very blue eyes and the broad, solid build of a football player. He wore a nice black suit, and there was the slightest of clefts in his chin.

I slopped hot coffee all over my hand.

"I'm sorry," he said in a deep, pleasant voice. "Did I surprise you?"

Now I was trying to pretend that the spilled coffee on my skin didn't hurt. "Sorry! Oh. Oh. Oh, no. No, of course not. Sorry. Sorry about that!"

That was word for word what I said.

The man broke into a slow smile.

My heart burst into flutters.

"Are you new here?" he asked.

"Yeah. Yeah, yeah, I am." I forced myself to take a deep breath and try to speak lucidly. "I'm Ashley."

"John. John Cooper. Glad you're on board."

That was it. That was our entire conversation, and the only conversation we had for the first month I worked at the firm.

It was enough though.

I returned to my office, ignoring the burning sensation from hot coffee all over my hand. I pulled out my little planner—a paper one since I can never make an electronic planner work for me—and I wrote this sentence on the very last empty page.

I'm going to marry John Cooper.

Silly, I know. The kind of foolish romantic gesture a teenage girl might make.

But I was convinced it was true. It felt like a deep abiding knowledge that descended on me from on high.

And I believed it still, three years later, as I was riding up the hotel elevator on my way to my second evening with Sean Doyle.

My heart belonged to John Cooper. But my body, at least for tonight, belonged to Sean.

Two entirely different things.

There was safety in that. Safety in the fact that ultimately it didn't matter that Sean had built up impenetrable walls around his heart—around the deepest parts of himself—

and that I'd never be able to scale those walls or bring them down. I didn't want to.

I just wanted to have a good time for the next few hours.

That meant I had as much power in the hotel room as Sean did, even though he was the one who had drawn up the contract and fortified himself with artificial barricades.

I knocked on the door.

As I waited, I had to admit to myself that I was really excited about tonight, about seeing Sean, about having sex with him again. He didn't have to be the love of my life.

He was really good in bed.

I frowned when he didn't open the door.

I knocked again, my heart starting to sink at the possibility that he wasn't even here.

He hadn't left a message downstairs at the front desk, which was what he was supposed to do if he'd decided not to show up or if he had a scheduling conflict.

But he wasn't responding to my knock.

I was breathing in ragged little pants and washed with a deep chill of disappointment as I knocked the third time.

He wasn't here.

He hadn't been as excited as I'd been.

He'd found me boring last time, not worth another evening.

And here I was knocking on the door like a pitiful fool.

The door swung open suddenly, making me gasp.

"Sorry," Sean said with a little quirk of his mobile mouth. In the past two weeks, I'd forgotten how sexy his mouth was. "I thought I could get the shower done before you got here."

I was almost shaking with surprise and relief.

He was standing across the threshold, wearing nothing but a white towel wrapped around his waist. His skin was slightly damp, the moisture glinting on his firm flesh, lean muscles, and scattering of hair. This man wasn't nearly as classically handsome as John Cooper, but damn, he was incredibly sexy.

"What's the matter?" he asked, his green eyes sharp and observant as they studied my face.

"Nothing," I said, making myself smile in a confident, relaxed way. "Why would something be wrong?"

"You look strange." He stepped aside to let me into the room.

"Thanks very much," I said tartly.

There was a bottle of red wine on the table near the window, just like there had been last time. I headed for it immediately, thinking a glass of wine was exactly what I needed.

Sean grabbed my hand and pulled me back around to face him. "What's up, Ash?" he demanded.

"Nothing," I said, starting to get annoyed by his persistence. Hadn't he ever heard of just letting something go?

He pulled me closer to him and said softly, "Tell me."

I rolled my eyes and pulled my hand out of his grip. "That kind of bossiness might work with your employees, but it won't work on me."

One of his eyebrows arched up in a quizzical expression. "It won't?"

Damn it. *Damn it.*

I couldn't quite hold back a laugh.

He smiled, clever amusement warming his face. "There's that sense of humor. I noticed it at the meeting on the first day we met. You thought I was funny and had to fight not to show it."

He was exactly right. I'd thought it would be a betrayal of our client to laugh at Sean's ironic little comments, so I'd struggled to keep a straight face.

Evidently, my struggle had been unsuccessful.

"If you're going to be smug and annoying," I said coolly, "then maybe I made a mistake in coming here again."

"I don't think you made a mistake." He adjusted his towel, which was sliding very low on his hips.

I tried not to leer. "Why did you take a shower?"

"I had a four-hour meeting this afternoon in a stuffy conference room. I wasn't in fit state for company."

I'm not sure why, but I kind of liked that he got hot and sweaty—just like any other man—and that he was willing to admit it. "Oh yeah? I thought you weren't supposed to let the other guy see you sweat."

"You're not. That's why I kept my jacket on, which made it even hotter." He chuckled. "But the other guy was in worse shape than me. He was drenched."

"I guess that's what you call a successful meeting then." I was still standing in the middle of the floor, near the foot of the bed since Sean was blocking my way to the wine.

"Successful, yes. But I definitely needed a shower afterward."

"I thought you weren't here," I admitted without thinking. "When it took you a while to answer the door."

His lips parted slightly as enlightenment washed over his face. "Ah. I see."

I arched my eyebrows in an attempt at lofty disinterest. "You see what?"

"That's why you were all stiff and breathless when I opened the door. You thought I'd stood you up."

I gasped. "I wasn't stiff and breathless!"

I was breathless now because Sean had taken a step closer to me and his eyes had taken on a heat I remembered from two weeks ago.

"Yes, you were," he murmured. "You were preparing yourself for disappointment."

"I wouldn't have been *that* disappointed."

This was an outright lie. I'd been looking forward to tonight for two weeks. I'd been anticipating, imagining, fantasizing about it. Far more often than I was comfortable with.

He moved even closer, so we were less than two inches apart. "Really? *I* would have been disappointed if you hadn't shown up."

My cheeks flushed, and for some reason I was nervous again—nervous that I was so excited, that I was already so aroused. "Maybe I should take a shower too."

"Did you have a four-hour meeting?"

"No."

"Then you don't need a shower." He gave me that sultry smile and pulled his towel away from his body, dropping it on the floor.

I blinked as my whole body surged in exhilaration. He was already hard. Still feeling compelled not to show how excited I was, I asked lightly, "Just what exactly were you doing in the shower?"

"I was anticipating," he whispered into my ear.

My whole body clenched. Arousal hit me so hard and fast that it actually ached.

Before I knew what was happening, he'd grabbed me, walking me backward until the back of my legs hit the foot of the bed. Then I was tumbling down onto the mattress, and Sean was on top of me, his green eyes hot and his body warm and naked.

"I heartily approve of the skirt," he murmured, sliding my skirt up to my hips to free my legs.

I'd worn a skirt today, which I almost never did since no one else in my office wore them. I hadn't even done so consciously, although I realized now I'd worn it in the hopes that I might be sexier for tonight.

Before I could respond, Sean was kissing me.

His kiss was deep and urgent, and I realized he'd been honest about his anticipating our time together. He must have been looking forward to it as much as I'd been. There was no other explanation for his eagerness now or his lack of preliminaries.

It worked for me. I was already flushed and wet, arousal pulsing between my legs. I was still wearing my heels as I wrapped my legs around Sean's body.

He yanked my blouse out from my skirt as he kissed me and then fumbled around until he'd unbuttoned it. My jacket had already been hanging open, and he didn't even bother trying to get it off. He kissed his way down my neck to my breasts and then nuzzled and nipped over my bra until I was gasping and arching up into his mouth.

It was all happening so fast that it should have been a problem for me. I just don't go from my normal self to hot arousal in so little time.

Not normally anyway.

It was probably because I'd spent so long looking forward to tonight. The imagination is a powerful aphrodisiac.

For whatever reason, I was already ready for him, my fingers digging into his back as I rocked shamelessly beneath him. Before I knew it, he'd slid down my panties and pulled them off over my shoes.

When he lifted his head, he gazed down at me with a look of pleased possessiveness, as if he enjoyed seeing me so turned on from so little. He said, "Don't move."

"What?" I stared up at him as he stood up. I was sprawled there on the foot of the bed, my clothes half on and my legs splayed apart, no underwear or anything, and he was telling me not to move.

"Don't move," he said again, walking over to one of the nightstands.

I'm not sure why, but I obeyed him. I didn't move. I was confused and uncomfortable, but there was something incredibly hot about staying in this position because he'd said so.

He returned in just a moment, and I finally saw what he'd been doing.

A condom.

He'd been getting a condom.

Good thinking, really.

He tore the packet open and rolled on the condom before he lowered himself on top of me again, bracing himself on one arm and using the other to position himself at my entrance.

I moaned as he eased himself inside me, pleased that he was breathing as loudly and unevenly as I was.

I wrapped my legs around him as he started to thrust.

29

There was nothing graceful or controlled about us. It was all raw, urgent, almost clumsy. He pushed into me with fast, hard thrusts, and I squeezed my legs around him as I rocked up with shameless enthusiasm. I had to be poking into his ass with my heels, but he obviously didn't care. Both of us were grunting like animals, shaking the bed, working ourselves up to release.

Under normal circumstances, I'd never have been able to come with so little foreplay, but all my fantasies and anticipating over the past two weeks had evidently taken care of that for me. I was already close. As the pleasure tightened, I suddenly felt out of control, so I reached above my head with one hand and fumbled for purchase on the bedding.

"That's right," Sean murmured thickly, his mouth very close to my ear. "You're about to come already, aren't you? Fuck, you're so hot, so good. You're gonna come so hard."

There was no rational reason for his words to get to me the way they did, but my whole body clamped down in pleasure as he spoke. Then I was coming, tossing my head against the mattress and trying to bite back the loud cry that was bursting out of my throat.

His motion grew tighter, harder, as I shook through my orgasm. He was grunting loudly now, right in my ear, and I loved that he sounded so out of control.

I was still working through the spasms of my release— which went on much longer than I would have expected— when Sean started to jerk and shudder too. He didn't try to rein in his exclamation of release the way I had. He didn't have the same inhibitions.

We were both sweating and panting as we finally reached completion. For a minute he pressed his weight into me. His naked body was so hot, so heavy, and it was relaxing so deliciously. It matched exactly what I was feeling myself.

But, after a minute, I realized how heavy he was. And my back was aching from the position, hanging halfway off the bed. Plus I was still trapped in my clothes, and they were damp and uncomfortable. And my hair was sticking to the sweaty skin of my face and neck.

I groaned and shifted beneath him.

He grunted in response but didn't move.

"Sean." I gave him a little poke in the side.

"All right. All right. I'm moving." He didn't move immediately, but he did eventually. He heaved himself up, rubbing his face and smiling down at me.

I didn't like how smug his expression appeared. I frowned. "What are you grinning at?"

He was taking care of the condom, but his eyes were still on me. "You're looking deliciously…"

My frowned deepened. "Deliciously what?" I supposed I looked like an embarrassing mess, all hot and disheveled and debauched.

"Sated," he said.

I rolled my eyes. "You're looking pretty sated too, you know."

"No question about that." He reached down with his free hand and helped me stand up. When I gasped and grabbed at my back, he asked, "You okay?"

"Yeah. Not the most comfortable of positions, if you want to know the truth, but I'm sure I'll live."

He grinned at me and then went to the bathroom to get rid of the condom and wash up. When he came out, I was smoothing out the wrinkles in my skirt.

His eyebrows drew together. "You're not leaving already, are you?"

31

"No, I don't think so. Why?"

"You left right afterward last time."

He was right, but it had just been twenty minutes since I'd arrived. I didn't want to leave yet, and I was quite happy that he clearly didn't want me to. I wasn't sure what I was supposed to do now though, so I said the first thing I thought of. "Well, I don't think I will this time. I think I might take a shower."

He nodded, his face relaxing. "Good plan. The hotel has excellent water pressure."

I was chuckling as I went into the bathroom, closed the door, turned on the shower, and took off my clothes.

I was about to step into the shower when I heard Sean's voice from outside. "Ash?"

I was standing in the bathroom completely naked, and his voice surprised me. I acted on instinct, reacting quickly. I gave a little squeal, slamming my hand down on the bathroom door to hold it closed.

It was only after I did so that I realized how foolish it was.

There was a pause from outside the door. Then he asked, "Are you all right?"

"Yeah," I called breathlessly. "Fine."

"What's going on in there?"

"Nothing." My cheeks were hot. I might wish to be some sort of cool, modern woman—the kind who had casual affairs and walked around hotel rooms completely naked—but I would always end up embarrassing myself. "I just didn't want you to come in."

I heard him chuckling from outside the door. "I wasn't going to come in."

"Good."

He was still laughing. "I was just wondering if you were hungry. I'm going to order room service. Do you want something?"

"Oh. Yeah. Yeah, that would be great."

"What do you want?"

"I don't know. What's good here?" I was still naked in the bathroom, still holding the door closed, just in case.

"All their steaks are great. And the salmon is really good." He still sounded like he might be laughing at me.

I loved steak. *Loved* it. All my health-conscious friends shook their heads at me for eating red meat, but it had always been my favorite thing. I was used to people disapproving of it, however, and it would involve trying to decide which kind of steak to choose. So I went with the easier option. "Salmon would be great."

"With what side?"

I almost groaned. This was just too many decisions for me to deal with when I was about to step into the shower. "I don't know. What's good?"

"The risotto?"

"Perfect. Thanks!"

Relieved, I was finally able to get into the shower and wash away the sex and the self-consciousness and remind myself that I didn't have to put on a show for Sean.

He liked to have sex with me, and it didn't really matter what he thought of me otherwise.

~

As Sean had said, the shower was excellent, and I stood under the hot spray for a long time before I soaped up with the expensive body wash provided by the hotel. I did my best to keep my hair out of the water since I didn't want to spend the rest of the evening with sopping wet hair.

When I got out, I dried off, put on one of the thick white hotel robes, and stared at myself in the mirror.

My cheeks were flushed, and my lips looked redder than usual. My skin was as pale as usual otherwise, with a faint dusting of freckles on my nose. My hair—despite the sex and the steam from the shower—didn't have even a hint of a sexy wave. It was straight as a stick, like normal.

I tried to fluff it out, ever hopeful, but I gave up when it did no good. It was smooth and shiny, but it would never have any sort of body.

When I left the bathroom, Sean was sitting at the table, reading something on his phone. He'd pulled on a pair of soft black pajama pants, but that was all he wore. He must have brought them with him, and I made note of that for next time. If he could bring something comfortable to wear in the room between rounds of sex, then so could I.

He glanced up and gave me a quirk of a smile. "You want some wine?"

"Yeah. That would be great." I went over and sat in the other chair at the table while he poured me a glass of merlot.

I sipped it, not sure what I was supposed to say now that the sex was over and the food hadn't yet come.

"How's your week been?" he asked casually, putting down his phone.

It was a normal, innocuous question—something anyone might ask. But his eyes were holding mine and he looked like he might be genuinely interested, so instead of just saying "fine" I answered him for real. "Not bad. Kind of boring. Now that my big job is done, it's a bit of a letdown to get back to normal."

"Your big job?"

"Yes. My big job. Helping to make that deal with you was the biggest job I've ever done."

He nodded as if he understood this. He clearly didn't question that any project involving him and his company was an important, noteworthy one. "What does your normal work look like?"

"One home closing after another."

"I guess that's to be expected when you're in property law."

"Yeah. Of course. And I'm the low man on the totem pole at work, so I get all the little stuff. It's really not that bad." Even when it got boring, I enjoyed my job and considered myself lucky to have it.

"Why did you go into property law instead of something else more exciting?"

"I don't know. Most lawyering isn't that exciting."

"But why property?" He'd almost finished his glass of wine, and his eyes were focused intently on my face.

I opened my mouth and closed it again. Then decided there was no reason not to tell him. "When I was in college, my grandparents lost their home. They'd lived in it for fifty years, and a big land developer swooped in and bullied and cheated them out of it." I sighed, closing my eyes as I thought about the memory. "They were... devastated. They didn't have an advocate—at least not one who knew what he was doing— and so they didn't get anything closer to a fair deal for the house. They just... lost it. I know everyone says that possessions and property shouldn't be that important, but a home is different. A home is special. They were both almost eighty, and they lost their home. They never really got over it."

Sean was quiet for a moment, clearly thinking about what I'd told him. "So you went into property law so you could help people like them."

"Not immediately. I knew in college I wanted to be a lawyer, but I'm not sure I even knew what it entailed. I just had these vague daydreams of defending people in court. When I got to law school, though, and I had to start making decisions, what happened to my grandparents was what decided me."

"Are they still alive?"

"My grandmother is. She's in an assisted living place now. She's doing okay, but…" I didn't finish. I wasn't sure how I was supposed to finish. It felt strange and almost dangerous to have shared something so personal with Sean.

He didn't say anything. He just took his last sip of wine and put his glass down quietly on the table.

Wanting to do something to get the emotional pressure off me, I asked, "What about you?"

"What about me?"

"Why did you become a property developer? Your family is all cops, right?"

"Yeah. My father and grandfather and three cousins and my sister and both brothers."

"Wow. So why didn't you do that too?"

"I don't really know." He didn't sound like he was avoiding the question. He seemed to mean what he said. "I think I just wanted to do something different. And I wanted to make money."

I laughed. "Nice."

"I know it sounds mercenary, but it's true. I think money is a prime motivator for a lot of people's career decisions, particularly when you grow up without a lot of it."

"Yeah. Yeah, I know."

"I was always the smartest of the bunch, and my parents wanted me to go to college, which no one else in my family ever did. I majored in business without really knowing what I wanted to do, and then I started an MBA program. It was only then that I figured it out."

I tried to imagine Sean as a college student, as a graduate student, and I simply couldn't do it. He wore competence and authority like his suits—like it was part of him. "And what does your family think about it? Are they disappointed you didn't follow the family tradition?"

His thin, expressive mouth did a little twist. "They were all right. My dad was disappointed, and I got a lot of snide comments from my brothers, but no one really held it against me. My grandmother was always really supportive. *Follow your heart, boy. Always do your own thing.*"

The last two sentences were clearly in the voice of his grandmother—spoken in a thick Irish brogue.

My eyes widened as I chuckled. "Does she really talk like that?"

"Oh yes."

He didn't speak with even a trace of an accent. His speech was clean, uninflected, and it occurred to me then that he might have worked to make it so.

I asked, "So your family is really Irish?"

He arched his eyebrows very high. "You know my name is Sean Doyle, right?"

I laughed even more. "Of course. I've got Irish in my family background, but it doesn't really impact who we are. So I didn't know how... how close the Irish heritage was for you."

"Very close. *Very* close." He looked like he'd say more, but there was a knock on the door then, and he got up to let in room service.

The server put the dishes on the table with the glasses, utensils, napkins, condiments, and a bottle of sparkling water.

Sean signed the bill and waited until we were alone in the room.

"Thanks for dinner," I said, lifting the silver cover off my plate. The salmon, risotto, and vegetables looked delicious.

Sean's ribeye looked even better.

We were quiet as we started to eat, and I found myself wondering how I would feel if I'd been eating dinner in a hotel room with John rather than Sean.

It would be better. Surely it would be better. I couldn't imagine anyone else being as smart and funny and interesting as Sean, but it would have to be better if I was with a man I loved.

Right?

I tried to imagine John wearing nothing but pajama pants and chewing a bite of steak across the table from me. It was an attractive image but strangely blurry around the edges.

"What are you thinking about?" Sean asked, breaking me out of my reverie.

I felt almost guilty, like I'd been caught doing something naughty. "Nothing."

"You're thinking about the jackass, aren't you?"

I gasped, as much in surprise as indignation. "No! Of course not. Why would you say that?"

"Because you had a dopey expression on your face," Sean said with a hint of that smug little smile.

I gasped again and stiffened my spine. "I was not dopey! And he's not a jackass!"

"Oh yes, he is."

"You don't even know him."

"I told you last time. I know everything I need to know about him. You're the one who doesn't really know him."

"I work with him every day."

"And let me guess. This week, he brushed against you in the hallway, making your heart go all pitter-patter." His voice was low and amused and not at all bitter. He was teasing me but in a way that proved he liked me and that didn't offend me at all.

I rolled my eyes, trying very hard not to smile. "No. He's been out of the office for a few days."

"Sick? Didn't you rush to his side with chicken soup and sympathy?"

"He's been out of town."

He'd taken some vacation days and had gone to the Caribbean. He didn't have a serious girlfriend, but I was pretty sure he'd taken a woman with him.

If I hadn't had my evening with Sean to look forward to, I would have been seriously depressed about it.

I kept telling myself it didn't matter though. John wasn't in love with me. He had women in his life that weren't me. He didn't have someone special though, so he wasn't a lost cause.

Sean *was* a lost cause.

He'd given his heart once, and that was clearly all he had in him to give.

At least I wasn't stupid enough to fall for Sean the way I had for John.

"He's not who you think he is," Sean murmured, without as much teasing in his tone.

I met his eyes across the table. "You have no idea who I think he is."

He nodded as if acknowledging the words, and I was relieved when he let the subject drop.

I didn't mind him teasing me a little for having a crush. I was the one who'd told him about the love of my life when I was drunk last month. But I didn't want anyone to doubt my feelings were real.

I knew it was crazy, but my feelings *were* real. I had absolutely no doubts about them.

"Sometimes," I said softly, slowly, "you just know."

Sean was silent for a moment, and his expression grew very deep, very serious. "Yeah. I know."

He did know.

He'd been in love too—and far more deeply than I'd ever been.

He'd been so in love he was going to marry the woman—and she'd been cruelly taken away from him.

He was such a charming, clever man that it was easy to forget the tragedy that shaped the core of who he was now.

"Anyway," I said, trying to break the mood, the tension, since it made my chest feel tight, "There has been no brushing up against him in the hallway this week."

"Oh well," Sean said with a little smile, the teasing awakening in his eyes again. "Maybe next week."

My eyes dropped to Sean's steak, which was halfway gone now. It was a thick cut and very dark pink in the middle.

My salmon was excellent, but I craved that steak the way I would chocolate.

"You're wishing you'd gone with the steak, aren't you?" Sean asked, once again managing to read my mind.

"No, of course not. The salmon is delicious."

"But it's not steak." He was smiling just a little as he carved another bite off his ribeye and speared it with his fork.

He raised his hand, waving the bite in front of me. "You want a bite?"

God, did I want a bite.

"Maybe," I admitted.

He extended his arm, clearly expecting me to eat the bite off his fork. I leaned forward, and I couldn't fail to see the look in Sean's eyes as I pulled the steak off his fork with my mouth.

He was thinking about sex again. The heat was unmistakable in his eyes.

And now I was thinking about sex again too.

I moaned as I chewed the steak, which was tender and succulent and delicious.

"Good, isn't it?" Sean's voice was huskier than before.

"Mm hmm."

"Next time you'll have to get the ribeye too." He cut off another piece and offered it to me like he had before.

What could I do but take it?

That fire in his eyes was really turning me on.

By the time we finished eating, we were both aroused. He pulled me out of my chair and over to the bed, taking off my robe as he did so.

I had nothing on beneath it, so I was completely naked the way he had been earlier. He went a lot slower this time, spending a lot of time on foreplay, kissing me all over, teasing me until I was flushed with arousal from my face to my thighs. I was moaning and gasping in an embarrassingly eager way, but there was no way I could stay quiet.

The man just knew what he was doing.

We were more securely on the bed this time as he put on a condom and bent up both my knees. He pushed both my legs toward my chest as he entered me, and I was clutching at the headboard frantically, feeling out of control and trying to hold on in any way I could.

He wasn't in any sort of a rush. He took his time, even though his face was tense with something like hunger. He fucked me until I came and then came again, nearly sobbing with it as my body shook and shuddered. Only then did he come too, letting himself go in a hot rush of release.

I was half gasping and half giggling from how good it had been as he rolled off me. I straightened my sore legs, but the discomfort only made me feel even sexier.

"Pretty good, huh?" Sean was flushed and smiling as he eyed my obvious satisfaction.

Honestly, he looked pretty satisfied too.

"Oh yeah." I smiled back at him, still trying not to giggle. "That was better than good."

I couldn't ever remember coming like that in my life, but I wasn't about to admit such a thing to him.

He was already smug enough.

As he went to the bathroom to take care of the condom, I barely had enough energy to roll over and reach down onto the floor to grab my robe and put it on again. Then I collapsed back on my pillow, smiling up at the ceiling like an idiot.

Sean came back, leaning over to snag his pajama pants. He sat on the edge of the bed to put them on and then stretched out beside me.

He didn't try to pull me into his arms or touch me in any way. That would have been unnatural—an unspoken lie that both of us would have recognized. But he was still smiling as he turned on his side to look at me.

I still hadn't caught my breath, and my body felt deliciously limp and heavy, like I could just sink into the bed.

"You look like you're feeling pretty good," he murmured.

"I am. I definitely am. The only thing that would make it better is chocolate."

He chuckled and reached for the phone. "We can take care of that."

I had to suppress more giggles as he ordered us dessert from room service.

So it was the best evening I'd had in a really long time, and I didn't even feel strange about it like I had two weeks ago.

This was good. It was enjoyable for both of us, and neither one of us was going to get hurt—since we'd set the boundaries so clearly from the very beginning.

Yes, it would be better with a man I loved, but I wasn't going to pass up something that felt so good.

We weren't each other's first choice. Both of us knew it.

But second best wasn't bad at all.

THREE

Two months later, I walked into the lobby of the same hotel. I felt particularly pretty and sophisticated today in a skirt suit and a new pair of heels. It felt like men were checking me out, which didn't normally happen for me.

I wondered if it was my imagination or if I was becoming sexier somehow.

As I walked past the check-in desk, the middle-aged man who was always there on Wednesday evenings stopped me. "Excuse me. Ms. Simon?"

I blinked at the sound of my name and turned toward the speaker with a questioning look. This was my sixth Wednesday night meeting Sean at this hotel, and none of the staff had ever done more than nod and murmur good evening to me as I entered.

My heart nearly stopped as I realized the man had a message for me.

From Sean.

This couldn't possibly be good.

"Mr. Doyle is running late," the man said. "He asked me to give you a key."

Enlightened—and immensely relieved that Sean was still planning to show up—I took the key card and continued up to our regular room.

The hotel room was immaculate and strangely empty without Sean waiting there for me like normal. There was a bottle of red wine waiting with two glasses on the table, as there had been every other night.

I wondered how late he would be.

I could sit down and drink a glass of wine. I could pull out my laptop from my bag and clear out some emails. Or I could take a hot shower and be nice and clean and fresh when Sean arrived.

The last option was most appealing, so I pulled out the slinky, dark blue pajama set I'd bought over the weekend (especially for tonight), slipped off my pretty new heels (pinkish-buff-colored with cute little straps), and headed for the bathroom.

After I turned the water on to get hot, I pulled my hair back into a messy bun and dropped my clothes onto the floor, feeling almost decadent—like I wasn't just a normal girl with a normal job living a normal life. I loved the specialty bath wash the hotel provided—deliciously scented with lavender and honey—and I scrubbed up and rinsed off at a leisurely pace.

I wondered what Sean was doing.

He probably had a meeting run late or else something urgent came up at work.

I was going to be very disappointed if the front desk called up to tell me he wasn't going to be able to make it after all.

I'd been waiting for two weeks for tonight. I didn't want to miss out.

When I felt an unexpected blast of cool air, I turned to see what caused it. I squealed loudly when I saw a man getting into the shower with me. I raised my hands instinctively to beat him off.

You understand I wasn't thinking through any of this. All I'd processed was the sudden appearance of a man where I hadn't been expecting one.

"Hey," Sean said, laughing as he grabbed at my flailing wrists. He was as naked as I was. "I expected a warmer welcome than this."

I relaxed immediately, flushing with embarrassment and the aftermath of my shock. "You scared the crap out of me!"

He was still laughing. "I can see that. Who did you think was getting into the shower with you?"

"I don't know. I thought you were running late."

He moved so he was completely under the shower spray, the water soaking his short brown hair and streaming down his high cheekbones, strong chin, and sexy mouth. "I was. But I rushed over so you wouldn't start without me."

"Start... without...?"

I didn't finish the stilted question because he'd pulled me into a kiss.

I had no objections to kissing him. In fact, it was one of my favorite activities. No one kissed like Sean Doyle did—with those clever lips, agile tongue, and dedicated skill. But I'd put my hair into the bun on purpose, and I didn't want him to pull my head under the water, so I backed away, saving my hair from getting soaked like his.

He frowned when I broke the kiss and reached for me again. "Why are you all standoffish?"

"I'm not." I giggled as I evaded his hands. "I just don't want my hair to get wet."

"Why not?"

I stared at him through the steam-thickened air. "Why not? Do you have any idea what it's like to go around with wet hair as long as mine? It takes forever to dry, and it gets everything wet."

He frowned and stepped forward, pushing me back against the shower wall. "Fine. If you insist on focusing on practicalities, how's this then?" He kissed me again, and this time I didn't have any desire to pull away. My head was safely away from the fall of water.

"Not bad," I murmured against his lips.

"Not bad? That's all you can say after two weeks without kissing me?"

"What did you expect me to say? That your kiss is the most incredible thing I've ever experienced in the universe?"

He nuzzled the side of my face, his tongue darting out to taste my skin in little, unexpected licks, each one causing a quick jolt of pleasure. "That wouldn't be a bad start."

I couldn't help but laugh, even though my hands were busy feeling their way down his broad shoulders and straight back until I'd reached his lovely, firm ass.

If I haven't mentioned it before, he had a very fine ass.

The nicest ass I'd ever gotten my hands on.

"Your ego is totally out of control, you know," I told him.

"Yeah?"

I gasped when he cupped my breasts with both hands and twirled my nipples with his thumbs. "Yeah," I managed to reply, arching into his palms. "Your…"

"My what?" he asked thickly when his skillful fondling distracted me from finishing my sentence.

"Your…" I had absolutely no idea what I'd been trying to say.

"My ego." He pushed against me, and I could feel that he was completely hard already, his erection big and firm as he pressed it against me.

I grabbed for him eagerly. "Your ego," I agreed. "It's way too…"

One of his hands had slid down my side to my hips and then snuck between my legs. Then his fingers were exploring in a way that made my whole body tighten.

He'd tilted his head to kiss his way down my neck, but I could hear a smile in his voice as he murmured, "My ego is way too…?"

My hands were still wrapped around his erection. "Way too… big."

"I've never had complaints about my ego before." Then he lifted his head and kissed me on the mouth again, and I surrendered to it, to him. As we kissed, I stroked and squeezed him, and he rubbed me intimately with one hand at the same time. The water was beating down on his back, misting over onto me, and my body was slick and warm. Everything felt so good and hot and sensual that I was moaning helplessly into the kiss.

I hadn't had a lot of foreplay yet tonight, and our position didn't allow him optimal access to the necessary parts of my body—whereas both my hands were working him over enthusiastically—so he got going first. After a minute or two, he jerked his mouth out of the kiss and let out an uninhibited groan.

His body was tightening palpably, and he'd braced his free hand against the shower wall, pushing into it hard.

I was quite familiar with his body now, and I knew what he liked. I picked up the speed of my pumping and watched as his face twisted in response. He groaned again and slammed his hand against the wall, as if he were trying to hold himself back.

I was almost as excited watching him come as I would have been coming myself. I was flushed and panting and breathless, and my whole body pulsed with arousal. I couldn't look away from his face.

He'd had his eyes closed as he reached the edge, but he suddenly opened them again, meeting my gaze as his body started to shake.

So he was looking at me as he came, and it was strangely unnerving. Exciting, but unnerving.

He groaned in pleasure as I felt him pulsing beneath my hands, and then he came all over my belly.

I wasn't actually a fan of a man getting semen all over me, but since we were in the shower, it wasn't unpleasant. As he gasped, muttering under his breath how good it had been and holding himself up against the wall, I moved under the spray to wash him off me.

I'd just gotten clean again when he grabbed me and pulled me into a wet hug.

I was surprised by the gesture, but I had no objections. It felt warm and good and real and not just because his body felt so nice against mine.

"For a guy with an ego as big as yours," I said in a lilting voice, "you sure do come easy."

He chuckled, his body shaking deliciously against mine. "I've been waiting for this for two weeks."

That was nice to hear. There wasn't love between us, but there was mutual pleasure, and it seemed to get deeper every time we got together.

"Me too," I admitted.

"Then let's see how easy you can come."

His voice had changed—he was able to focus more now that he'd come the first time—and he turned my body around so I was facing the shower wall. He placed one of my hands and then the other against the tile so I was bent slightly at the waist, braced against the wall.

My whole body throbbed at the position, and I stayed where he'd put me.

But I turned my head to look at him over my shoulder. "You're not going to try something as crazy as shower sex, are you? Because that's not going to be comfortable for me. If you're going to fuck me, we need to get out."

He shook his head. "I'm going to fuck you all right, but I'm going to do it with my hands."

I'll admit it. My whole body throbbed a few times at his words.

He caressed me from my shoulders to my breasts and then down my sides to my hips. He spent a lot of time on my bottom, which was prominently displayed in this position.

My butt has never been the best part of my body. It wasn't nearly as nice and tight and firm as his was. But he seemed to like it anyway as he squeezed and stroked.

I was aching with arousal and trying not to make embarrassing sounds by the time his hands finally moved between my legs.

He penetrated me with two fingers—I wasn't very wet because of the steam and hot water, but it wasn't uncomfortable—and he used the other hand to rub my clit.

I gasped and pushed against the wall as I felt a climax tightening.

"There you go," he murmured thickly. "You like that, don't you?"

Of course I liked it. It felt so good I couldn't hold back whimpers. My hips were moving of their own accord, trying to intensify the sensations.

"That's right," he was saying, sounding very pleased by my responsiveness. "Move just like that. Faster now. Let me see how much you want it."

I wasn't just moving now. I was shamelessly riding his hand, my breasts and bottom jiggling with my eagerness. My eyes were squeezed shut, and I was making rhythmic little grunts.

"You're going to come so hard, aren't you? Just from my hand. You're going to be screaming by the time I'm done with you."

I was afraid he was right, but it felt like a challenge, so I bit my lip to try to hold back the sounds I was making.

It didn't work. It all felt too good. I was bouncing my body now, braced against the wall. My breasts were slapping against my chest, and it felt so raw, so naughty, that it intensified my pleasure.

"You're going to come when I say to, aren't you?"

I didn't normally like that kind of thing. When I had an orgasm was my business—not some bossy man's—and I wasn't really keen to follow anyone's commands. But I heard myself sobbing out, "Uh-huh, uh-huh," in what was obviously an affirmative.

I wanted to come so much. I knew it would be so good. My whole being was on the edge of a precipice, waiting for him to push me off.

Then he did. "Now, baby," he rasped. "Come now."

I might have screamed after all—just a little. The orgasm overwhelmed me completely, and there was no way biting my lip was going to hold it back.

I kept riding his fingers, pushing my bottom back against his hand. I can't imagine how I must have looked—

naked and bent over and out of control like that—but I was too caught up in sensation to even care.

My lungs and cheeks were burning as the last of the spasms finally worked their way through me. Sean was stroking me gently, and he didn't stop until my grunts and moans had finally quieted and I'd grown still.

I was still staring at the wall, but I knew he was smiling behind me.

He was very pleased with himself.

He liked how he'd gotten me to throw off my normal inhibitions. It had given him some sort of macho thrill.

My body was still shuddering with the aftermath of pleasure, so I could hardly begrudge him his pride.

He helped me straighten up, and I rinsed myself off again, smiling at Sean but not quite able to speak intelligently yet.

After another minute, he turned off the shower and we both dried off. I was reaching for my pretty new pajama set when he stopped me. He was hard again, even though it hadn't been very long since he'd come the first time.

He took my hand and led me out to the bedroom, grabbing a condom on the way. Then he pulled me into a kiss, and we ended up toppling over onto the bed. He turned me over onto my back, positioned himself between my legs, rolled on the condom, and entered me.

He fucked me slowly and rhythmically, my legs bent up against my chest. I'm not sure if I actually came again, but the whole thing felt amazing—raw and deep and intensely pleasurable. We didn't talk the way we normally did, but it didn't feel like we needed to.

It just seemed like we were in sync. We knew each other's bodies now, and so we didn't need to discuss what worked and what didn't.

We knew what worked.

We knew how we worked together.

I was gasping with pleasure and rubbing my palms over his back when his motion finally grew more urgent. He was going to come. I knew the signs. I squeezed around him as he fell out of rhythm and huffed his way to another climax.

Both of us were smiling and relaxed when he rolled off me. I was tired, sated, and a little bit hungry.

We lay on our backs, side by side, smiling at each other until Sean finally got the energy to sit up and take care of the condom.

"Steak tonight?" he asked me with his irresistible quirk of a smile.

"Oh yeah."

That was another great part of our evenings together.

It wasn't just great sex.

It was also great food.

Can you blame me for looking forward to it every other week?

Can you blame me for occasionally wishing we could do it a bit more often?

~

When I'd finished eating a salad, loaded baked potato, and a lot of my ribeye (Sean finished it for me), I got up to use the bathroom, and then I flopped down onto the bed, feeling tried

53

in that pleasant satisfied way you only feel when you've had a really good time.

Over dinner, we'd talked about a show on Netflix that Sean had told me he'd liked the last time we got together. In the past two weeks, I'd watched all three seasons, so we had a great time discussing it and speculating about what would happen in the next season.

We'd fallen into silence now though, and I stretched out on the bed, my head on the pillow. It wasn't even nine o'clock yet. Our evening wasn't over.

I wasn't sure why I was suddenly experiencing a strange heavy sensation below my belly.

Not desire or anything like it.

It was almost poignant, which didn't make any sense at all.

Sean had been checking his phone while I was in the bathroom, but now he put it down and stood up from the table where we'd eaten. He was wearing a pair of blue-gray sleep pants, and I automatically ran my eyes up and down his body.

He must work out a lot. He was naturally lean, but no one was born with lovely, tight muscle development like he had. His stomach was perfectly flat.

He had a small white puckered scar on his side—from the bullet that had shot him two years ago. The night his fiancée had died.

I'd never mentioned it or paid it extra attention, but it was hard not to look at it occasionally.

"What?" he asked, evidently noticing my stare.

"I wish my stomach was as flat as yours," I said. It was a silly thing to say, but I was trying to ignore that poignant feeling and not wanting him to know I'd been looking at his scar.

He chuckled and lowered himself onto the bed beside me. "I've got to say that I'm glad you don't have my body. I wouldn't find it particularly enticing."

I couldn't help but giggle at his words. I reached over to rub my hand over his abs, loving the feel of the firm muscles and tight skin, the way it rose and fell slightly with his breathing, the hair that trailed under his waistband. I avoided caressing his scar the way I wanted to. "I don't want your body. I'd just like a perfectly flat stomach like yours."

My stomach wasn't flat. It wasn't particularly large, but it definitely curved outward.

"I like that you're soft," Sean murmured.

I frowned at him. "What?"

"I like that you're soft," he repeated with an arch of one eyebrow. "Your body, I mean. I like it soft."

I rolled my eyes but couldn't hold back a smile. "You say all the right things, don't you?"

"Was that the right thing to say?"

"Don't act all innocent with me. You know exactly what you're doing, trying to butter me up that way."

He rolled over on his side and gave me a smile that was half-wicked and half-intimate—very appealing. "And what am I doing?"

"You're saying exactly the right thing."

"Very convenient then since it happens to be true."

I wondered if it was true. I wondered what the other women he'd been with were like—whether they were gorgeous model types with perfect bodies and hips that weren't overly rounded like mine.

Sean was a man very experienced with women, so he very likely knew exactly what would make women feel best about their bodies. He was also a decent man and more generous than most people would expect, so he might go out of his way to smooth over the insecurities of the woman he was presently fucking.

But still… I wondered what the other women he'd been with were like.

His fiancée had been gorgeous and slim—and she'd trained in ballet. She wasn't anything like me.

I wanted to ask him about her. And about the other women he'd been with.

I couldn't though. I'd signed a contract that said I wouldn't.

I felt that little twisting in my gut again and tried to ignore it. It didn't matter that there were things I couldn't ask, things I couldn't know. I didn't need to have a heart-to-heart with Sean to have a very good time.

"How's your mom's back?" Sean asked, rolling over so he was lying on his back the way I was.

"It's better," I told him, pleased and surprised that he remembered I'd mentioned my mother's back had gone out a couple of weeks ago. "She's moving around fine now. I almost wish she still had her back to complain about since all she's talking about now is my sister's wedding."

"Oh really? Your sister is getting married?"

"Yeah. She just got engaged two weekends ago, and my mother is obsessed with wedding plans already. Every time I call her, that's all she wants to talk about."

"Is she your only sister? Older or younger?"

"Yeah. My only sister. Younger. By two years." I sighed and tugged down the top to my pajama set. It was made like a camisole, and the slippery fabric kept inching up, baring my belly.

"And how do you feel about her getting married?"

I turned my head to check his expression, but his face was mild and interested. He didn't seem to have an underlying motive for the question other than curiosity.

I gave a little shrug. "I'm happy for her. Of course. I'm pretty reasonable about these things, and I'm not going to get all uptight about my little sister getting married before me. She's never been very career-minded like I am anyway. All she's ever done is try to get married. The guy she's marrying is okay but nothing special. I sometimes wonder..."

"You wonder what?"

"It sounds kind of mean, and I don't intend it to be that way. But I wonder if she's mostly marrying him to get married. He'll treat her fine, I'm sure, but she doesn't seem very..." I shook my head. "She doesn't seem like she's head over heels about him. But he has a good job, and she wants to get married, and she's twenty-six now, so she thinks it's time."

Sean was studying my face, as if he were analyzing every little flicker of my expression.

His fixed gaze made me a little self-conscious. I lowered my eyelashes. "I don't know. Maybe I'm wrong. I hope she'll be happy."

"I think more people do that than we realize," Sean said after a thoughtful pause. "Marry someone because they're there and because they want to get married. A lot of those marriages work out just fine."

I nodded, letting out a long breath. "And a lot of couples who are passionately in love at the beginning end up in divorce in less than five years. I know. I'll hope for the best for her."

"If it's a mistake, you'll have to let her make it. There's nothing you're going to be able to do at this point."

"I know. I wouldn't even try. And I don't have any reason to assume it's a mistake. It's what she wants, so I'll be happy for her. And I'll put up with months of her and my mom talking about nothing else."

He chuckled. "Weddings do seem to overwhelm everything else. Lara was always—"

I went very still at the sound of his fiancée's name. He'd never mentioned her before in my presence—in casual conversation or in anything else. I only knew Lara was her name because of what I'd read in the newspapers.

I didn't say a word. I didn't prompt him to continue after he'd cut himself off. I felt ridiculously nervous—and a little excited—as I waited to see if he'd finish.

He was staring at the ceiling, and his tone changed—softened, got slightly hoarse—as he finally continued, "Lara talked about the wedding all the time too."

I had absolutely no idea what to say, so I just murmured, "Yeah."

It felt like a wound in him had broken open—just a crack but enough to cause blood. He wasn't trying to confide in me. He'd never do that. He'd just been into the conversation and a reference to Lara had slipped out.

It seemed to bother him. I could feel a different sort of tension in his body—emotional, conflicted.

I wanted to soothe it away, but it wasn't my place, and I had no idea how to do it anyway.

Finally I decided the best thing to do was change the subject, move us past it. So I said lightly, "My sister is all excited because they were able to reserve this old farmhouse and orchard for their wedding. It's a really nice venue and doesn't even cost a fortune."

Sean seemed relieved at the return to normal, and he turned his head to face me again. "Is the ceremony going to be outside?"

"Yeah. That's the plan."

"Where would you get married, if you had a choice?"

"I don't know."

"Really? You haven't daydreamed about where you and your jackass are going to tie the knot?"

I gave him a swat on his belly at this teasing reference to my beloved John Cooper, but I couldn't take it seriously. He always referred to John that way.

He laughed. "You didn't answer the question."

"I'm not some silly teenage girl!" I reached over to swat him again, but he grabbed my wrist so I couldn't.

"You still didn't answer the question," he said, his fingers still wrapped around my wrist. "You do have a few daydreams, don't you?"

"Of course I do," I admitted, flushing slightly but not as embarrassed as I would have thought I'd be.

"So in these daydreams, where are you marrying the jackass?"

I rolled my eyes since he refused to ever say John's name, but I thought through the answer to his question. "I'm kind of traditional, so it's usually a church."

"Yeah. I don't even want to imagine what my grandmother would say if I suggested I get married anywhere but a church." He was smiling, the way he always did when he referred to his grandmother. He must love the old lady a lot. "She thinks destination weddings are for heathens."

I giggled and rolled over onto my side, tugging down my top again. "I wouldn't mind a destination wedding, I guess. It would just depend on the situation."

"And I guess it would also depend on the jackass's preferences."

"Right."

"Is he still dating that woman?"

For almost a month, John had been dating someone. It was longer than I'd ever seen him date anyone else, and it had been worrying me a lot. But at Sean's question, I was able to smile. "No. They broke up. He told me."

"Ah." Sean's green eyes rested on my face with that same light scrutiny I saw so often—as if he were interested in what was going on in my head but didn't have a lot invested in it. "That's a relief then, I guess."

"Yes."

"He actually told you himself?"

"He did. I didn't even ask. He just brought it up himself."

John had been a little more chatty with me this week than he usually was. I wasn't foolish enough to put too much stock in it—it was probably just a passing thing—but it made me happy.

"Sounds promising."

I glanced over at what sounded like an edge to his voice, but there was nothing but his normal teasing smile on his face. I shrugged. "When you're caught up in an unrequited love situation, there are a lot of ups and downs."

"I guess so."

"You've never felt unrequited love before, I suppose."

"Sure I have."

My eyebrows went up. "Really? Who?"

This was a question right on the edge of breaking the clause in our contract about no talk of previous sexual relationships, but it didn't appear to bother Sean at all. His mouth twitched. "I was desperately in love with my third grade teacher. Mrs. Haversham. Damn, she was hot."

I laughed. Then I noticed that Sean was rubbing his neck absently as he talked, and it made me curious. "Does your neck hurt?"

"What?" He lowered his hand. "No, not too bad. I think I slept on it wrong last night. It's nothing."

He was clearly shrugging off the discomfort, and it interested me. He evidently didn't like to show any sort of weakness, even something as mild as a sore neck.

I wondered if he was naturally that way or if he'd learned to put on the invulnerable front because of his business.

"Turn over," I said, pushing myself up to a sitting position on the bed, inspired by something I could do for him.

"What?"

"Turn over. I'll rub your neck."

"You don't have to rub my—"

"I know I don't have to. I want to. So stop whining when someone offers to do something nice for you."

He rolled his eyes, but he was half smiling as he turned over onto his stomach.

I scooted over so I could reach him easily and start to massage his neck.

I'm not any sort of expert at massage, but I'd found you could do pretty well just by searching for the tension. Sean groaned as I pushed into the tight muscles and pressure points in his neck and the base of his skull, so I must have done a pretty good job.

"Do you get professional massages?" I asked as I worked.

"Nah."

"Why not?" He had plenty of money and surely could fit in a couple of massages a week. I couldn't think of any reason for him not to, especially since he really seemed to be enjoying even my amateur attempt.

"Never seemed worth the time."

"Why not?"

"If I want to relax, I'll watch TV or have sex."

I chuckled at this as I moved my hands higher up into his head, massaging his scalp through his hair. "But you only have sex every other Wednesday." I paused. "Right?"

I didn't even think about the question until the words were said, and then I immediately regretted them. I'd assumed I was the only person Sean was fucking. That was how the whole setup with the contract had made it seem.

He was certainly the only person I was sleeping with.

But at his silence, I was suddenly nervous. I grew very still, my fingers still tangled in his hair.

Then finally Sean murmured hoarsely, "Yes, I only have sex every other Wednesday night. You're not having sex with anyone else, are you?"

"No! No, of course not!" I was flushed, but it was with pleasure as much as embarrassment now. I was so incredibly relieved to confirm that I was the only one he was seeing.

"Then why did you ask if I was?"

"I wasn't thinking. I didn't really think you were. I was just thinking that if you only have sex every other Wednesday, then that still leaves a lot of relaxing that needs to be done. So a massage now and then wouldn't be a bad idea." I'd started working on his neck again, pleased to feel that the tight muscles were starting to loosen.

"Do you get massages?"

"Yeah, occasionally. As a special treat."

"You're really good at that."

"Thanks." That was very nice to hear.

He started moaning again as my hands lowered to his shoulders, and ridiculously it was starting to turn me on.

I didn't let it distract me though. I massaged my way down his back and then moved back up to his neck again. Eventually his whole body had loosened, and his groans were sounding a lot sexier than they had at first.

After a long time, he turned over without warning, and I discovered the reason for the sexiness of his groans.

He was hard.

Despite my own arousal, I tsked my tongue and said, "Are you serious? You get turned on by an innocent backrub? No wonder you don't want to get massages regularly. That would be pretty embarrassing."

He chuckled and pulled me over him so I was straddling his hips. "It would only happen if you were the one giving me the backrub."

"Uh-huh." I tried to sound lofty and skeptical, but I was having trouble not rubbing myself against him.

"Take off your top," he told me.

I stared at him.

"Take it off," he instructed. "I want to see you."

I did as he said, wondering why his words were turning me on even more. As I tossed the top onto the floor, Sean's eyes raked over my bare breasts and tight nipples. My breasts jiggled with my motion, and his nostrils flared slightly.

"Now the pants," he murmured.

This was a little more awkward since I had to lift up my legs to get the pants off over my feet, but I managed it eventually, hoping I hadn't looked too unsexy.

Sean didn't seem to think so. He was leering at me quite nakedly.

"Do you want to ride me?" he asked.

I did. God help me, I did.

I reached over to the nightstand for another condom, and then I pulled down his pants enough to free his erection and roll it on. Then he helped to position me above him, and I lowered myself onto his hard length.

Being on top is usually not my favorite position. It makes me self-conscious, and I'm never quite sure how I should move. But I loved the way he was gazing at me so hotly, and I was so turned on that I didn't even debate with myself the most attractive way to get going.

I rocked over him, slowly at first but then with more urgency. He held on to my bottom possessively, helping to hold me in place, and his eyes roamed from my face to my shaking breasts to where he was pumping in and out of me.

It didn't take me very long to come, and then he told me to keep going, so I rode him until I came again.

Then he rolled us both over so he could take control, and I reached up to hold on to the headboard for purchase. It was all feeling so incredibly good that I came again as he did, my body nearly flying apart as I banged the headboard against the wall.

As I came down, my throat hurt and my lungs hurt, and I was sore between the legs. But it felt like every sliver of tension in my body had been deliciously released.

When I could move again, I went to the bathroom to clean up and splashed water onto my face. Then I pulled my pajamas back on and went back into the bedroom.

Sean was still sprawled out where he'd collapsed earlier. His skin was damp, and his face was flushed and sated.

He reached out to take my hand and drag me back into the bed beside him.

"You've got to be crazy if you think we're going to have more sex," I told him.

"No more sex," he agreed. "It's going to be a while before I can get it up again."

I chuckled.

He let go of my hand, and I pulled the covers up over us since I was starting to feel a little chilly.

I'd rest a little before I left. A rest would be nice.

I closed my eyes.

It was a long time before I opened them again.

~

When I woke up, I was confused and disoriented. It wasn't dark in the room since lights were on in the bathroom and entryway, but everything felt strange and foreign.

I'd slept hard and really well. I hadn't dreamed or woken up or anything. And the bed was comfortable and cozy. But something was wrong. Something was definitely wrong.

I blinked a few times and lifted my head, discovering that Sean was sound asleep beside me, the covers pushed down to his waist and his arm slung over toward me.

Then I focused on the clock and discovered it was five twenty-two.

In the morning.

Five twenty-two in the morning.

I'd slept all night in bed with Sean instead of leaving like I was supposed to.

I sat up with a jerk and breathed until my mind was clear. Then I swung my legs over the side and started to get up.

Sean reached out and grabbed my pajama top to stop me. "Where... going?"

"I've got to leave."

"Don't leave... yet." He was clearly half-asleep, not conscious of what he was saying.

"It's almost five thirty in the morning, Sean. I've got to get home so I can get ready to go to work."

"Stay... with me." He still wasn't awake.

"I can't. I've got to go." I pulled my top out of his grip and made myself stand up, pulling my clothes on hastily

My heart was fluttering uncomfortably as I looked back at Sean in the bed. He'd rolled over onto his side and was breathing slow and even again.

He looked almost vulnerable, which Sean Doyle never was. And also strangely lonely in the bed all by himself.

I wasn't even sure why.

But I could hardly get back into bed with him. I had to drive home, shower and dress, and then get back into the city for work. I had an eight o'clock meeting this morning, and I needed at least twenty minutes to prepare beforehand.

So I left.

The night before would have to tide me over for two more weeks.

And Sean would have to get himself up whenever he really awakened.

I'd see him again in two more weeks.

That was the deal, and it was a good one.

It couldn't last forever. Sean and I weren't in love, and one day that was what I really wanted. Maybe even a wedding of my own—the kind I did sometimes daydream about.

As I rode down the elevator, an image came to me of myself in a beautiful wedding dress, walking down the aisle of an old church to a handsome, waiting groom.

This groom was nearly always John Cooper.

For just a moment, however, the image flickered, and I saw Sean in a tuxedo at the end of the aisle, gazing at me with awe in his eyes and with a quirk of that sexy mouth.

I shook the visual away immediately since it was ridiculous.

Sean wasn't groom material, and he never could be. He'd closed that door when his fiancée died, and he wasn't going to open it again.

I didn't even want him to.

I had with Sean exactly what I wanted. For now.

Sure, it wasn't my daydreams come to life, but second best could still be pretty damn good.

FOUR

Two weeks later, I knocked on the door to the same hotel room with a strange twisting below my belly.

I was nervous, and I had no idea why.

I'd done this same thing six times before—come to this hotel after work to meet Sean on every other Wednesday—and I knew what to expect now. There was nothing new or different about this evening.

I was still talking myself into this piece of common sense when the door opened and Sean stood in front of me.

He wore an expensive suit and a red-and-gray tie. His five-o'clock shadow was thicker than normal, and his hair was slightly damp at the edges—like he'd been sweating or he'd splashed water onto his face.

I wondered which one it was.

When I just stood there staring, he arched his eyebrows. "Are you debating whether to come in or not?"

"No, no." I felt silly—for both my nerves and for my momentary distraction—so I smiled at him self-deprecatingly. "Just admiring your manly physique."

I'd thought the ironic compliment would make him chuckle, but he didn't even smile. He stepped aside to let me in, his eyes focused on me but not even a trace of his lip quirk in his expression.

Something was different.

Something was wrong.

"What?" he demanded softly when I studied him, trying to figure out his mood.

"Nothing." I gave him a blithe smile and walked over to the wine, mostly for something to do. I poured some into each of the two glasses and handed one to him.

He took it and then sipped, his green eyes still resting on my face. He still hadn't smiled.

He hadn't *smiled*.

It felt deeply significant, and it made my stomach twist even more. I sat down in one of the chairs at the table and drank my wine, trying to figure out Sean's mood from the posture of his back and the tension of his jaw.

I simply couldn't read his mind, so the only way for me to find out was to ask. "Did you have a bad day?" I asked lightly, hoping it would come off as casual conversation.

Sean had walked over to the big window and was staring out at downtown Boston. But at my question, he lowered his glass from his lips and glanced over at me. "No. Why?"

An edge to his tone made me wish I hadn't voiced the question. "I don't know. Just asking."

I sat in silence, searching my mind for something that would explain his strange, tense mood.

I'd been a little uncomfortable emotionally after the last time we were together. There was no rational explanation for it, but that previous evening had left me feeling... jittery. Maybe just because we'd fallen asleep together, and we'd never done that before.

Maybe Sean felt something similar. He'd come up with this whole sex contract on purpose to avoid any sort of intimacy or emotional entanglements. Maybe he thought lines had been crossed last time, and so he was taking a dramatic step backward tonight.

Maybe.

That didn't feel right though.

When the silence had stretched out longer than I was comfortable with, I put down my glass. This was ridiculous. I wasn't going to sit here and feel awkward and uncertain. That wasn't what our relationship was supposed to be about. "Do you want to do this tonight?"

His eyebrows went up again as he turned to look at me. Still no trace of a smile. "What?"

I stood up. "I asked if you're up to this tonight. Because if you're not, it's really fine. I can just—"

He moved over so he was in front of me. "You want to leave?"

"I don't want to leave. I was asking if you wanted me to. You seem…" I made a vague gesture with my hand, hoping it would encompass all the tension I was sensing in him.

"I seem what?" he asked in that same soft, hoarse voice. His expression was almost a challenge, as if he were daring me to insult him.

I didn't want to insult him. I didn't want to do anything like that. I gave a little shrug. "I don't know. You seem like… you've had a bad day."

I'd circled back to the only explanation that made sense to me.

Everyone had bad days now and then. Even Sean Doyle.

"My day has been fine," he gritted out.

"All right then."

"Are you going to leave?"

"No, I'm not going to leave if you don't want me to."

"Good."

"Good."

We stared at each other for a moment. Then Sean put down his wineglass and took my head in his hand, pulling me into a hard kiss.

After that, things went the way you'd expect them to go. We kissed for a minute or two before it got too intense to stay on our feet. Then we ended up on the bed together. Sean rolled over on top of me, his hands busy as he continued to kiss me.

I was wearing a pantsuit today—I'd bought a few skirts in the past couple of months, but I hadn't had enough energy to wear one that morning. (I wasn't sure why, but wearing a skirt always took more energy than wearing pants did for me.) Sean got rid of my jacket quickly and unbuttoned my vintage-looking blouse without even breaking the kiss.

He was good at multitasking.

I kicked off my shoes and unbuttoned and unzipped my trousers, and then Sean was able to push them off over my legs. Then his kissing moved down from my mouth.

His hands slid up to my shoulders and then along the lines of my arms, his fingers wrapping around my wrists. He moved my hands up above my head and held them in place for a moment, as if he wanted me to keep them there.

The move stretched out my body, and he lifted his head to stare down at me, breathing raggedly.

I stayed in the position he'd put me, desire coiled tight between my legs but my heart beating erratically. Despite his transition into sex, Sean was still in that strange mood. There was more than just arousal in his face right now.

It was hunger but also something deeper, something conflicted, something aching.

I had no idea what it was, so there was no way for me to answer it.

I wrapped my arms around his neck, wanting to respond to the need I felt in him in any way I could. But Sean just moved my arms back to where he'd put them before, stretching my body out beneath him.

He stared at me for a long time before he lowered his face to my neck. He kissed and licked his way from my neck to my breasts, and I was gasping and arching up into his mouth when he reached around to unhook my bra.

I was nearly naked now except my little white lace panties, and he was still wearing all his clothes except his shoes, which he'd taken off before I'd even gotten there. I normally wasn't too fond of his arrangement—me being the only one naked—but I was too distracted by everything else to have a problem with it tonight.

My body was already torturously aroused, and I still didn't understand Sean's mood.

His eyes were raking over my body. When I shifted with the need to ease the throbbing of my arousal, he slid his hands up and down my arms, like he was making sure I stayed in position.

Then he finally lowered his mouth to my breasts. He kissed and nipped and suckled until I was whimpering helplessly. Then his mouth moved even lower, skimming over my belly. He got so close to the top of my panties that my hips bucked up involuntarily, instinctively seeking his mouth.

He'd never gone down on me—just like I'd never done it to him. I'd told him that first evening I wasn't comfortable with it until I got to know someone better.

I knew him better now. I wouldn't have had any complaints if he'd moved his mouth between my legs. He didn't though. He just slowly slid off my underwear, his eyes devouring the sight of the skin he bared.

Then he lifted his body up, repositioned, and lowered his head back to my breasts. He kissed and caressed me until I couldn't lie still. Once, my hands flew up to grab at his hair, trying to hold him in place, but he moved them back above my head so I had to clutch at the bedding instead. The whole time, he didn't say anything.

That was one of the things that was so unusual about tonight. Sean was so silent.

He was a talker—in bed and out of it. He was never so wordless, never so quiet. The thought distracted me for a minute until he spread open my legs and stroked me with his fingers.

I was wet. Very wet. Embarrassingly wet.

My body wanted him so much it was out of my control.

He usually smiled when he discovered this proof of my desire, but he didn't tonight. He fondled me until I was on the edge of orgasm, gasping and fisting my hands in the bedding. Then he pulled his hand away.

I gave a frustrated sob and tried to grind myself against him, but I'd lost the momentum of climax now and was still achingly aroused. I was writhing beneath him as he returned to my breasts, and after a few minutes I discovered I was begging him in broken gasps. "Please... please... I need... Oh God! Sean, please!"

Finally—finally—he lifted his head, and my skin broke out in goose bumps as he stared down at me again for a long time. I have no idea how I must have looked, stretched out in the position he'd placed me, my spine arching involuntarily, my hips impossible to hold still, my hair messy and occasionally sticking to my damp face.

I felt sexy and helpless and deep and needy and so incredibly vulnerable.

And I still had no idea what Sean was feeling right now.

"Sean, please," I whispered. "I need you to fuck me now."

My words must have broken through his emotional tension because his features twisted slightly and he reached over to the nightstand for a condom. He was still fully dressed in his suit and tie, but he undid his trousers, freed his erection, and rolled the condom on.

Then, very slowly, he moved into position, parting my thighs wide and bending up one leg and the other so my knees were almost reaching my chest. He seemed to like that position the best.

He slid inside me with aching slowness, and when he started to thrust, it was just as slow. He built up a rhythm, rocking my body with his motion and staring down at me with those haunted eyes.

It felt so good and so torturous and so exactly what I wanted that I was mumbling out breathless pleas for him to take me, fuck me, make me come hard. At one point, I reached up to tug at his suit jacket, but he just moved my arms back to their former position. So I clung to the bedding and wondered why I loved it so much, needed it so much—letting him do this to me.

It took a long time because he kept his rhythm slow and even, but eventually my body couldn't hold back anymore. I shook and sobbed through a long, deep orgasm, and he didn't stop or slow down as my body clamp down ruthlessly around him. He fucked me until I came a second time—just as powerful, just as long-lasting.

I was hoarse at the end of it, tears streaming from my eyes.

He'd been watching me the whole time—ravenously gazing down at my urgent responses to him—but something must have struck him about my tears because he paused and asked thickly, "You okay?"

"Yeah," I gasped, my fingers still fisted in the sheet above me. "Yeah, I'm good."

I was more than good, but I wasn't sure how to express that he'd just given me the two best orgasms I could remember.

"You want more?" he asked, sweat beaded on his forehead and the bridge of his nose.

"Yeah. More. So much more."

He pulled out of me, and I was about to object until I realized he was just repositioning us. He lifted my legs so my ankles were on his shoulders and he leaned forward, bending my body in half as he entered me again.

I made a strangled sound as I felt him sinking farther inside me.

"Okay?" he asked breathlessly.

"Yeah. Good. Good."

He was deep. So deep. Much deeper than usual.

Despite his rigid control, I didn't think he could last long in this position.

I was right. His breathing had become thick and fast, and when he started to thrust, it was in short, choppy strokes.

He was too deep for me to come again, but it didn't hurt. It all felt incredibly good. Deep and raw and slightly uncomfortable and like he was so far inside me he was fucking my soul.

I'd never experienced anything like it before.

I couldn't move my hips, folded in half like this, so all our motion was his. He pushed into me fast and hard and kept grunting like an animal each time he did.

It took me a minute to realize that his grunts were actually my name. "Ash... Ash... Ash..." He said it over and over as he built up toward climax.

Soon there was no way I could keep my hands above my head, so I reached up to tangle my fingers into his hair. I held on to him that way, and this time he didn't try to move them back. His face was contorted with pleasure and tension and effort and something else as he reached the peak.

He let out a loud bellow as he came—uninhibited, totally out of control—and he jerked his hips a long time as he worked through the spasms of his release.

It took him longer to come down than normal, and I stroked his hair and back as he did, feeling so strange, so helpless, so confused.

When his muscles finally relaxed and his expression softened, he rolled off me with a long groan.

I carefully untangled myself and straightened my legs.

They hurt. All of me hurt.

And all of me felt good at the same time.

I had to lie still for a minute before I was able to stand up. I was completely naked and stiff and sore, and I gasped when my back caught as I rose.

"Okay?" Sean asked, opening his eyes at the sound I made.

"Yeah. I'm fine." I was pleased that I sounded almost normal. "You want me to take care of that?" I gestured to indicate the condom he was still holding.

He nodded and I took it from him, throwing it away in the bathroom.

I had no idea what to do or say, so I was pleased when I thought of a reasonable activity. I grabbed my bag and told him, "I'm going to take a shower."

He nodded, acknowledging my words. He still hadn't moved from where he was sprawled out. It was like he'd collapsed at the release of tension.

I gave him one last look before I went into the bathroom.

I closed the door and stood there for a long time, thinking.

Sean hadn't smiled. Not once since he'd opened the door for me.

And that sex had been amazing, but it had also been...

Something was wrong with him, and I didn't know what.

I turned on the shower, waited for the water to get hot, and then stepped under the spray. I stayed in the shower for a long time, letting the hot water clean and then soothe me.

But I was thinking the whole time, and when I finally got out, I had an idea.

With a towel wrapped around me, I reached for my phone from my bag. I pulled up a browser and entered a few words.

Then I read the first news article that was brought up, looking specifically for the date.

I'd been right.

The idea that had come to me in the shower had been correct, and I now understood what was wrong with Sean, what explained everything about how he was behaving tonight.

Tonight was the anniversary of his fiancée's death.

Two years ago tonight, she'd been shot on a downtown sidewalk as they'd been walking home. He'd been shot too.

Tonight was the night.

No wonder he was acting like he was hiding a wound.

My throat hurt so much I could barely breathe, and I had no idea what to do about what I'd just discovered. Instead of putting on the pretty pajama set I'd brought with me, I put on a bathrobe.

My clothes were still on the floor of the bedroom.

When I came out, Sean was still sprawled out on the bed. He hadn't moved at all.

"Are you all right?" I asked softly.

He opened his eyes. "Yeah."

I stared at him for a minute, and then I made up my mind. I reached down for my panties and then looked until I found my bra on the side of the bed.

Evidently, this caught his attention. "What are you doing?" he asked.

"Getting dressed," I murmured. "I'm going to leave."

He shouldn't have to try to act normal and entertain me tonight. He shouldn't have to hide what he was feeling. He needed to grieve. I was going to let him do that.

This made him sit up and swing his legs over the side of the bed. "What? Why?"

I met his eyes. Hesitated.

Something new twisted on his face. "Did I... hurt you? Did I hurt you before?"

"No. No. Not at all."

"Then why are you leaving?"

I sighed. "I know what tonight is, Sean. I'm going to leave so you can be alone."

His expression changed again as he processed this. And I was reaching for my trousers near his feet when I felt his hand on my arm.

I looked over at him, waiting for him to speak.

"Don't leave," he rasped at last.

My heart jumped very strangely. "But, Sean, you shouldn't have to worry about socializing with me tonight. I think it would be better if—"

"I want you to stay." The words seemed torn out of him. "Don't leave."

I let out a breath, blowing out tension I hadn't known was making my body tight. Then I sat on the edge of the bed beside him. "Okay."

He'd turned his head to study my expression. "I didn't hurt you? I know I was… I felt like I might have been rough."

"No! Sean, of course not. I would have told you if you'd been hurting me. I… It was really good for me." I sighed. "I really liked it."

"Okay."

We sat in silence for a full minute. Then I reached over and put my hand on his knee. "I'm really sorry about Lara," I murmured, my voice breaking on the last word.

I wasn't looking at his face, so I don't know what his expression reflected. But his voice was as soft as mine had been when he said, "Thank you."

~

We didn't eat steak that evening.

The restaurant downstairs had a specialty of lobster pasta in a wine cream sauce, so we both ordered that. It just felt like a night to do something different.

After he'd called down our order, Sean went to take a shower. He was in there much longer than normal. In fact, the shower had just turned off when I heard the knock on the door. I went to let our room service in and sign the bill (hoping

I'd left the size tip that Sean would have done since this was being charged to him), and the courteous server was just leaving when the bathroom door finally opened.

Sean came out with wet hair, wearing the same kind of sleep pants he'd always worn—a solid color in a soft material. His chest and feet were bare.

I didn't know what to say as he paused in the middle of the floor, so I finally just gestured toward the table where the server had left the tray. "You hungry?"

"Yeah."

I poured myself another glass of wine and topped off Sean's half-empty one. I felt nervous, strangely jittery, as I stared down at the plate.

It looked delicious.

I had no idea what I should say.

To distract myself, I sipped my wine. "I think I'm getting spoiled with this wine," I said at last.

Sean had just taken a bite, so he swallowed before he replied. "Spoiled?"

"Yeah. I used to just drink whatever someone gave me, but ever since I've been drinking the wine you have here..." I shook my head and smiled down at my glass. "I was at a friend's house over the weekend, and she had a bottle of merlot. It was regular grocery store wine—not the bottom shelf but probably no more than fifteen dollars for the bottle. The kind I used to always drink. And I..."

"Could tell the difference?" he prompted. For the first time all night, he gave a hint of his normal smile.

I chuckled. "Yeah. I could. It's a very strange thing to happen to me. I've never cared about wine at all."

He'd relaxed a little as I talked, and I realized he wanted the distraction. It wouldn't be insensitive for me to talk about light, easy things as we ate. In fact, it might be exactly what he needed.

So I kept talking. Not incessantly but enough to fill the silences between us. I told him a couple of stories about clients I'd met within the past week. I told him about new developments with my sister's wedding. She'd found out she was pregnant, and she wanted to move up the date for the wedding so she wouldn't be showing when she got married. So all their ambitious wedding plans were being condensed to less than three months, which to me seemed like a recipe for disaster.

Sean drank all his wine and poured himself another glass. Then he finished his lobster and pasta.

He didn't add a lot to the conversation, but his eyes were on me and he responded enough to sustain the conversation.

He looked a lot better when we were finished, and I was foolishly proud of myself for helping him—even in such a small way.

"That was really good," I said when I took my last bite. I hadn't finished everything, but I'd done pretty well for myself. "I don't even regret not getting the steak."

"Yeah. Me either." He swallowed the last of his wine. He'd had almost three glasses, which was twice as much as he normally drank.

I didn't blame him for wanting to dull his senses a bit tonight though. I would have done the same thing.

We sat and stared at each other across the table for another minute. Then I had to break the tension I could feel building again in the air. With a smile, I got up and went to use the bathroom.

I didn't really have to go. I just wanted to do something.

When I came out again, Sean had gotten up from the table and moved to stretch out on the bed, his head turned away from me so he could look out the window.

I crawled onto the bed beside him. I wanted to touch him, stroke him, since he seemed sad again, but I didn't think it was my place.

When I straightened my legs, I felt a twinge of soreness and sucked in a quick breath.

Sean turned to look. "You okay?"

"Yeah. Just a little sore. From before." I paused, then had to admit the truth. "That might be all the sex I'm up for tonight."

He nodded. Didn't look surprised or disappointed. "You would have told me if it was too much for you?" His eyes were very sober.

My lips parted at the question. "Of course. Of course I would have told you. I'm not the kind of girl to suffer in silence."

He gave another little hint of a smile, so I felt better.

"And I don't let guys do things to me that I don't want," I added.

He nodded and murmured, "Good."

He was such a decent guy. Even wounded and grieving tonight, he still worried about me. And I knew he meant it when he'd said it was good I wouldn't let a guy do something to me I didn't want.

Some guys wouldn't even think to ask. Some guys were too focused on putting their dicks wherever they wanted them, no matter what the other person needed.

Sean wasn't like that. At all.

"So any new developments with the jackass?" he asked after a minute.

He asked me about John every time we got together. I'd always thought it was because he liked to tease me—and I was still sure he did—but he wasn't in a teasing mood now. That meant he must genuinely be interested.

"Well, uh, not really, I guess."

His mouth turned down slightly. "What does that mean?"

"It just means that nothing significant has really happened, although he's talking to me more now than he ever did before."

"But he hasn't asked you out?" I couldn't understand the expression in his eyes when he voiced the question.

"No. Although we did eat lunch together on Monday. Just accidentally. In the break room. But..." I trailed off. It was starting to sound a bit silly that I was so excited about eating lunch with a guy.

Maybe I was kind of silly.

"But what?" Sean prompted.

I was still wearing the white hotel bathrobe, and I had to pull one side back up over my shoulder since it was slipping down. "But it was something. Or it would have been if I hadn't embarrassed myself."

I'd been planning to tell Sean about this for the past two days. In fact, I'd worked out the story in my mind several times, planning it out in a way that made it as funny as possible. I'd actually been looking forward to Sean laughing about it.

He wasn't laughing now though, so I wasn't sure I should go into it. It didn't match the feeling between us right now.

"What was embarrassing?" His eyes were still focused on my face, and it seemed like he really wanted to hear the story. So I told him.

83

"I was eating lunch in the break room," I began. "And then he comes to sit down with me since he was eating lunch too. He was asking me all these questions about myself, and I was happy about it. I don't know if you've ever felt this way, but there's this strange sort of excitement when you've wanted something to happen for a long time, and then it seems like it's happening. And you're in the moment, but it also feels like someone else is in your skin. And the whole world seems to be... shuddering—like it's a film, but someone isn't holding the camera still." I sighed and gave him an ironic smile. "I guess you've probably never felt that way."

"I have. I know what you're talking about."

My heart gave a little flip at this, for no good reason, and I had to force myself to focus on my story. I went on, telling him about the conversation and how I was so distracted that I'd taken a breath when I shouldn't have as I was eating my sandwich, and the bite of food went down the wrong way.

So I'd started to choke. My airway wasn't completely blocked, so it wasn't a crisis, but I couldn't stop coughing and I'd had to stand up as I tried to get control of myself, tears streaming down my face, smearing my mascara.

And poor John hadn't known what to do, so he'd gotten up and kept hitting my back like that would help until I could finally stop.

I played up the story as well as I could, making sure it was as funny as I could make it. It hadn't felt funny at the time. It had been genuinely embarrassing. But it had ended all right. John had seemed sincerely concerned, and he'd kept his hand on my back, sliding it down to just above my bottom in a gesture that felt more than supportive.

I didn't tell that part to Sean.

That part felt personal.

Sean enjoyed the story though. And he even chuckled as I reached the end, the only laughter I'd heard from him all evening. It wasn't his normal laugh. It was soft and hoarse and slightly poignant, but it was real.

And I saw exactly what happened after that.

He was laughing, his face almost relaxed, when suddenly it froze. His expression went completely still, and something pained and haunted filled his eyes.

I watched as it happened, and I knew exactly what it meant, how he felt.

For a moment he'd forgotten what had happened to Lara, and then he'd remembered all of a sudden.

Things always seemed to hurt more when you'd forgotten them for a little while.

He let out a rough breath and turned his face away from me, staring out toward the window again.

I had to do something. I had to comfort him in any way I could.

It had been two years. He would probably always miss her. But he was allowed to relax and enjoy himself. He didn't have to still feel guilty about it.

I reached over to stroke his bare chest. He didn't jerk away from my touch, so I kept it up, rubbing my hand over his collarbone, his flat nipples, the scattering of coarse hair, his firm abs.

Quite unintentionally, my hand moved over to his side to the scar from the bullet wound. It was pale and puckered and would always look damaged.

It was so wrong that his flesh had been ripped apart that way.

It was so wrong that his heart had been ripped apart too.

After a few minutes, he turned his head back to look at me. I was still lightly caressing his chest. It was the only thing I could think of to do.

My hand had strayed down to his belly and was idly playing with the line of dark hair above his waistband. Because my hand was low on his body, my eyes were too, so I saw when he started to get hard.

He was only partially erect, but it was noticeable under the thin fabric of his pants.

"Sorry," he said lightly. "I've been telling him there's no more sex tonight, but he doesn't always listen."

I giggled softly and moved my hand down to his shaft, holding it through the fabric.

He sucked in a breath. "If you keep touching him like that, he's never going to get the right idea."

I smiled then, suddenly thinking of something I could do.

Sitting up, I moved so I could have easy access to his body. "We can do something," I murmured.

"What?" His eyes were slightly narrowed from the way I was touching him, but he clearly had no idea what I was referring to.

"I can do something for you." I lowered my upper body so my face was very close to his groin.

He got it then. I could see quite clearly that he got it because his penis grew suddenly, visibly harder.

"Are you sure?" he breathed.

"Yeah." I smiled down at him, filled with pleasure at having thought of something I could do for him, something to address the way I was feeling, something that might make him feel a little better—if only for a few minutes.

I carefully stretched out his waistband and pulled down his pants, his erection bouncing slightly as it was freed.

Then I took him in my hands again, stroking him for a minute before I lowered my mouth.

Blow jobs had never been my thing. I'd given them to a couple of guys before—but only guys I was in serious relationships with. It had just never been something I enjoyed. In fact, one of my boyfriends had been generally a nice guy, but whenever I got his dick in my mouth, he'd start calling me all these dirty names, as if the position somehow called for the crude language.

Maybe some women got turned on by that sort of thing—which was totally fine—but it had felt demeaning to me. I hadn't liked it. At all. So I'd always disliked going down on him, and I'd been hesitant about it ever since then.

Tonight felt different though.

This was something I was giving to Sean. He wasn't taking it from me.

I was a little nervous, and my throat was aching with emotion, but I was also excited and tender, and I wanted to do this.

He hissed when I slid my tongue up and down his shaft, and his hips moved restlessly when I licked circles around the head. His hand had moved to the back of my head, combing through my loose hair and curling around the back of my skull.

He wasn't holding me there by force. It felt more like a caress.

I took him fully in my mouth and sucked a few times, and he moaned low in his throat. I sucked again, and his fingers tightened in my hair as he breathed. "Oh God. Oh God, Ash!"

My back was stretched uncomfortably, so I let him slip out of my mouth so I could rearrange my body. As I did, he reached over and untied my robe, slowly pulling the sides apart so he could see my breasts.

He was staring at me hungrily now.

I leaned over and took him in my mouth again. My blood was pulsing intensely, and I was filled with emotional tension I'd never experienced before.

As I sucked, I took his balls in one of my hands and squeezed them gently.

Soon—very soon—Sean was grunting low and soft, rocking his hips up toward me. I adjusted my rhythm and depth to accommodate the thrusts of his hips and breathed raggedly through my nose as the muscles of his thighs and stomach grew tighter and tighter.

"Oh fuck!" he gasped, reaching out to claw at the bedding with one of his hands. The other was fisted in my hair now. "Oh fuck. I'm… I'm…"

He was close to coming already. I could feel it, see it in his body. I kept sucking and squeezing as my own arousal throbbed achingly.

He was totally gone now, and I experienced a sudden flare of panic about what to do when he came. Should I let him come in my mouth—or should I move and let him come on my chest or something? What would he prefer? What would he expect?

These are the kinds of questions that always come to me at the worst possible times, even when I should be caught up in a moment. Maybe some women are completely confident about such things, but I have never been one of them.

As it happened, I didn't have time to make a decision. He was already coming, his body shaking with it and a long, unrestrained moan releasing from his throat. His shaft pulsed with his climax, and he ejaculated into my mouth. He'd come earlier though, so fortunately there wasn't that much semen for me to deal with.

I was panting as I wiped my mouth with the back of my hand and finally raised my head from his groin. I kept stroking him as he softened in my hand.

When my eyes moved to his face, I grew suddenly still.

His eyes were closed, and his features were relaxed. More relaxed than I'd seen them all evening.

But I could see a streak from a tear running from one eye down into his hair.

It stilled me. Filled me with too much. Far more emotions than I knew how to deal with.

I felt like I might burst into tears myself, so I did the only reasonable thing a person could do in my situation.

I got off the bed and went into the bathroom to clean up and rinse out my mouth.

I was aroused myself, but my emotions were a lot more powerful, and I didn't really feel like coming right now.

I had no idea what to do.

I stood in front of the mirror and breathed until I felt mostly calm again. Then I went back into the room. He was still sprawled out on the bed, his pants pushed down, his eyes closed, his body completely relaxed.

I walked around to his side of the bed to pick up the jacket to my suit. As I leaned over, he reached out to grab my hand.

I turned to look at him.

"Thank you," he rasped, holding my hand in his.

I swallowed hard. "You're welcome. I enjoyed it."

"I didn't just mean the blow job."

I gulped again, touched and emotional and so incredibly confused.

"Are you leaving?" he asked in a different voice.

"I... I don't know."

"Don't leave."

I let out a breath, those two words answering my lingering questions. "Okay. I won't."

So instead of picking up my jacket and getting dressed, I went back over to my side of the bed and crawled under the covers. Sean moved so he was under them too.

He'd rolled over on his side so his back was to me, but I still sensed a profound neediness to him, even in his silence.

So I did something very brave. An act of courage I didn't know I possessed. I scooted over and put my arms around him, spooning him from behind.

He raised one hand and rubbed my forearm, which made me think he liked that I was holding him this way.

He would never say so, but I was sure he did, so my nerves relaxed.

I didn't say anything else. We just lay together like that until his body softened completely and his breathing slowed down.

It wasn't that long before he was asleep in my arms.

It was a lot longer before I fell asleep myself.

Sean was sexy, handsome, funny, charming, ruthlessly intelligent. He was a success in every venture he'd ever tried.

In the past two years, he'd built barriers around his heart that would never come down.

He was strong and uniquely brilliant—making sure the world never thought he was weak.

But he would always be human.

And someone he loved had died.

~

We both slept through the night the way we had two weeks earlier, but I wasn't confused and disoriented when I woke up in the morning.

I felt heavy. Heavy and still emotional and absolutely terrified.

Sean was still asleep—his body warm and relaxed and irresistibly close to me—but it was almost six, and I had to get moving right away.

I got up quietly and got dressed in the dark, being careful not to wake him up.

I wanted him to sleep as long as he could.

I was slipping on my shoes when I heard him mumble, "Ash."

I turned to look and saw he'd reached a hand out for me, the way he had the evening before. I took his hand in mine, and he pulled me closer to the bed.

He'd opened his eyes to look up at me with a heavy, sleep-clouded gaze. "See you in two weeks?"

From the upward lilt of his voice, it sounded more like a question than a statement.

Could he actually be wondering if I wanted to meet up with him again?

"Yeah," I said. "I'll be here." Without thinking, I leaned down and pressed a soft kiss on his lips before I let his hand slip out of mine.

I shouldn't have done that.

It reflected something I shouldn't be feeling.

I had to get out of this room. Fast.

I grabbed my bag and left without another word. When I got into the elevator, I leaned against the wall, closing my eyes and telling myself to get a grip.

I was just feeling different because he'd been so sad and vulnerable last night. I'd feel this way about anyone I liked who needed comforting.

It wasn't anything more than that.

It couldn't be anything more.

Sean wasn't a man I was allowed to love—even if I'd wanted to. And I didn't.

John had always been the one I loved, and nothing about that had changed. Things were going well with him, and I had every reason to hope that they'd keep getting better.

I just felt close to Sean right now because he'd needed comforting last night.

I felt things for other people. It was normal and natural.

There was nothing for me to be terrified about.

If I couldn't stop thinking about Sean's face after he'd come, if I couldn't stop thinking about that single tear that had leaked out of his eye, if it made me want to run back to the room and hold him in my arms again—have him hold me too—then that was just a temporary response to the empathy.

It didn't mean anything.

And it certainly didn't mean that Sean's place in my life was changing.

After all, the world was what was, and Sean Doyle would always be Sean Doyle.

He'd always been my second best.

FIVE

Two days after that night with Sean, I asked John Cooper out.

I didn't normally do that sort of thing. In fact, I'd never done that sort of thing. I completely supported women asking men out whenever they wanted, but it didn't feel natural to me personally.

But after two days thinking about Sean and how we'd been together on Wednesday, I knew I had to take action before I got myself into an emotional tangle.

I'd made decisions a long time ago. I'd fallen in love with John on the first day I met him. And these confusions about Sean would fade away as soon as I was once again focusing on my priority.

John was my priority, and nothing about that had changed.

So I did something I never thought I'd do. I was desperate enough to take a real step. At the end of the workday on Friday, I stopped by John's office and asked if he wanted to grab some dinner.

I purposefully made it casual, spontaneous, like it wasn't a big deal. It *felt* like a big deal to me. I was so nervous my mouth was dry and my hands were freezing. I managed to get the words out though, and from John's friendly expression, I must have sounded basically normal.

He looked surprised, but he said, "Sure. I don't have any plans."

And that was it.

I was going to dinner with John after three years of wanting to.

We went to a little French place just down the block from work, and we kept it easy and casual.

The truth is, I was so focused on containing my excitement and not sounding like I was totally besotted or completely boring that the whole thing ended up being stressful rather than fun.

But it went fine. Perfectly fine. At the end, John leaned down to give me a little kiss just beside my mouth and said we should do this again.

I couldn't ask for more than that, after forcing the issue the way I had.

It felt like I was outside my body, watching myself say goodbye to him, and when I got into my car at last, I closed my eyes and groaned as I was finally able to relax.

It was good.

It was really good.

It was what I wanted.

And I could hardly compare one after-work dinner to my nights with Sean. True, the conversation hadn't been nearly so engaging. And true, I hadn't been able to relax and really be myself the way I was with Sean.

But I could hardly expect it to be the same.

I had no expectations of Sean. I knew exactly what we were together. With John, I was constantly hoping, waiting, wishing for something specific. It would change, get better, if we were in a real relationship.

I knew it would.

For one thing, I wouldn't be constantly overwhelmed with jitters whenever I was with him.

After reassuring myself of all these truths, I went home, feeling like the evening had been a success.

I'd thought I would think about John before I went to sleep that night, but my mind kept drifting back toward Sean.

I hoped he was feeling better.

I hoped he wasn't sad.

I hoped he wasn't still grieving for the woman he'd loved and lost.

I wondered how he'd act when I saw him again—a week from next Wednesday.

It seemed like a long time to wait.

~

Two Wednesdays later, I was leaving my office and thinking about Sean when a voice stopped me in the hall.

I turned to see John approaching me. He was leaving his office too, based on the fact that he was carrying his briefcase, and he joined me on my way to the elevator.

"You look really pretty today," he said with a slow smile.

I glanced down at myself, blushing at the compliment. I'd had enough energy to wear a skirt today—a charcoal-gray one—and I'd paired it with a cashmere sweater set instead of my normal suit jacket. I also had on my pretty pinkish-buff heels and a pearl necklace I'd inherited from my grandmother.

I felt like I could belong in *Mad Men*, and I kind of liked the feeling. John's was the fourth compliment I'd gotten today.

"Thank you," I told him. "That's nice of you to say."

"You want to grab a drink?"

I glanced at my phone to check the time and hesitated. I had forty-five minutes before my regular meeting time with Sean. "It will have to be quick. I've got plans later."

He didn't look concerned by this piece of news. If I'd hoped he'd be jealous by the possibility of my having a date, I was to be sorely disappointed. "No problem. We can go to the bar downstairs."

We'd had drinks a couple of times after work since that Friday I'd asked him out, and it was nice that he wanted to keep seeing me, even in such a casual way.

We went to the bar, and John bought us both drinks. He ordered me an Amaretto Sour without asking. I'd had one last time, but I was going to get something different today. He didn't give me a chance though, and it wasn't a big enough deal to make an issue of.

The bar was crowded for happy hour—filled with people like us who had just gotten off work downtown—so an intimate conversation was impossible. We chatted casually, and I smiled a lot, and I was pleased to discover I wasn't having such an out-of-body experience this time.

We both had two drinks, and by the time we were leaving, I could say for sure that John appeared interested in me. I caught quite a few admiring looks on his part.

I could also say for sure that he wasn't as smart as Sean.

Again, it wasn't a fair assessment. No one was as smart as Sean. I'd never met anyone else who could talk like him and think like him and put pieces together the way he did.

I didn't want or need John to be at Sean's intellectual level.

It was just an observation that I couldn't help but make.

I did feel a little strange, leaving John after getting another, slightly more lingering goodbye kiss and walking a block down to the hotel where I was going to have sex with Sean.

I'd never juggled two men before.

Women did it all the time. I had no commitments to either one of them. But it still felt odd to me.

If things got serious with John, I'd definitely end my Wednesdays with Sean. But we weren't there yet, and I didn't want to throw something good away if there wasn't a sure thing to replace it.

So I went straight to the hotel and arrived about ten minutes later than usual.

I knocked at the hotel room door and had to wait for a minute before he answered the door. I discovered why when I saw Sean was wearing a bathrobe.

He must have used the extra time to take a shower.

"You're late," he said by way of greeting. He wasn't frowning though. His mouth was turned up in a little smile, and his eyes were teasing.

I raised my eyebrows. "I think you've been late before, if I remember correctly."

"Did work run late?"

I went over to the table with the wine, and I dropped my bag onto the floor. "Just got a slow start coming over here."

I didn't add any more information. I'd intended to tell Sean that I'd had a drink with John earlier, but when the time came to do so, it didn't feel natural.

I wouldn't lie to him. That wouldn't be right. But I wouldn't volunteer the information that I'd been with John just now and that was why I was late.

I studied his face as he came to sit down in the other chair at the table, tightening the tie to his robe. He looked a lot better this week, without that haunting ache I'd sensed in him two weeks ago.

In fact, he appeared to be in a very good mood, if his dancing eyes and the twitching of his mouth was any indication.

"How's everything with you?" I asked, not sure how to broach the topic of his mood.

"Good. I'm good. No falling apart for me tonight."

My smile faded slightly. "You didn't fall apart last time."

He gave a half shrug. "Maybe. But I promise I'm good today."

"Good." I searched his expression, but he didn't seem to be beating himself up about his behavior last time, despite his self-deprecating comment.

He seemed... almost excited, like something good was going to happen.

I really wanted to know what it was, but I couldn't figure out a way for me to ask.

He went on, his face sobering a little as he spoke, "I think the two-year mark was particularly hard because... because I'm starting to forget." He paused and added, "Not that I'll ever forget her. I'm just not thinking about her all the time anymore."

I hadn't expected this kind of admission, and it made my heart jump almost painfully. I murmured, "I can understand that. It's been two years."

He nodded, not meeting my eyes now. "It's hard though. After holding on for so long. I go... days now without even thinking..."

He didn't finish the thought. He didn't need to.

"You can't feel guilty about that, Sean. It's been two years. Eventually everyone has to heal."

He nodded again, still not looking at me. He was silent a long time until he finally breathed, "I guess maybe I am."

I didn't know if he was talking to me or talking to himself. It seemed like a revelation to him either way.

"That's good." The words were too trite to answer what he'd said, but there weren't any better words in such a situation.

He lifted his eyes and smiled at me, and the emotion relaxed between us.

I sipped my wine, feeling relieved at the change in mood and just a little disappointed at the same time.

"I see you've got a *Man Men* thing going on today," Sean murmured after a minute, his eyes running up and down my body from my heels to my hair.

I actually gave a little gasp, so surprised was I at how he'd voiced something so close to my thoughts earlier in the day. "I wasn't intentionally going for that," I explained. "It just kind of turned out that way."

His little smile broadened irresistibly. "I like it."

"Thanks."

His eyes were still restless, running over my face and body. His smile turned into a thoughtful frown.

"What is it?" I asked, suddenly self-conscious, despite my pleasure at his appreciation for my appearance.

"You look... different. I don't know."

I wondered if he could somehow sense that my romantic dreams were starting to come true—at least the very first steps toward them. Surely that wasn't visible on my face. "I don't think I'm different."

"How would you know?"

"Well, I'm me. If anyone knows if something different about me, surely it would be me."

He was smiling again, as if he liked this slightly garbled response. "Maybe."

"Stop grinning like that."

"Like what?"

"Like a cat who got into the cream, as my grandmother used to say."

His green eyes transformed from amused interest to something deliciously heated. "Do you have something else in mind for my mouth to be doing?"

Despite my attempt to stay cool and lofty, my cheeks flushed hot. "I don't know. I could maybe think of a few things."

He stood up and extended a hand toward me. I reached mine out to meet it, and he pulled me to my feet. "Maybe you can show me what they are," he murmured.

I had no objections to that plan.

In fact, my whole body tightened with excitement.

We stood for a minute, holding hands, and I experienced the strangest clench in my chest. It wasn't nerves. It wasn't arousal. It was something else, and it was caused by the look in Sean's eyes and the way his warm hand felt around mine.

For a moment I was hit with another one of those flickering visions where I could see myself somewhere else. I imagined myself in a room like this, standing like this, but it was John who had that look in his eyes, John whose hand was holding mine.

I'm a pretty good imaginer, but I couldn't quite wrap my head around that visual. It didn't feel real to me the way this did.

The realization was troubling.

"What is it?" Sean asked softly, drawing his eyebrows together.

I smiled and gave my head a little shake, dismissing the vision and the reflections that had come with it. "Nothing."

He was still frowning, as if it bothered him that he couldn't tell what I was thinking.

As if he had any right to see into my soul.

He didn't.

We had a contract, and soul-searching wasn't one of the clauses.

"Ash?" he prompted.

My name was Ashley. No one called me Ash. No one but Sean.

"Nothing," I repeated, telling myself to get it together, or my enjoyable night of sex, food, and stimulating conversation would be ruined.

When Sean kept studying my face, I knew I had to move us past the weird moment. So I stepped closer to him, took his head in both my hands, and pulled him down into a kiss.

That got things moving in the right direction. Sean took control of the kiss almost immediately, sliding one hand down to the small of my back and pressing my body closer to his. When he deepened the kiss with his tongue, I lowered my hands to tug at my cardigan until I could slide it down my arms and drop it on the floor.

I wore a matching sleeveless sweater underneath it, and Sean took care of that one quickly by grabbing the bottom and breaking the kiss so he could pull it off over my head.

Today I was wearing a lavender bra, and Sean stared down at it for a few seconds with hot appreciation on his face before he pulled me back into a tight embrace.

We kissed for a few minutes, during which we managed to get rid of my shoes and skirt. Sean was still wearing the bathrobe, and I was starting to get rid of that when he grabbed me unexpectedly, swung me up into his arms, and carried me over to the bed.

I gasped at the sudden movement, clutching at his neck with both hands. I'm not particularly heavy, but I'm also not a wisp. I've got solid bones and muscles and some extra padding, and I'm not in the habit of men carrying me, even for a few steps.

In fact, I'd never imagined that anyone would.

So I was breathless and disoriented in Sean's arms like this. I wanted to tease him or make a joke or anything to sustain a light, familiar mood between us, but I couldn't think of a single thing to say.

Sean was smiling as he lowered me onto the bed.

I wanted to ask him why he'd done that.

I wanted to make some sort of ironic quip.

I wanted to do anything other than gaze up at him with wide, bewildered eyes the way I was sure I was doing.

Sean's smile turned into something almost tender as he lowered himself onto the bed and moved over me.

My breath—and any word I'd been trying to say—caught in my throat.

He kissed me, saving me the trouble of finding my voice, and then he raised his head to let his lips trail across my flushed face and then down to my neck. I wore my bra and panty set and my pearl necklace. Nothing else.

He clearly liked what he saw.

Once again, I opened my mouth to attempt something clever, but he kissed me before I could.

Not that I was in a fit state to think of anything clever to say anyway.

We kissed for a long time, the weight of Sean's body pressing into mine in a way I couldn't help but love. He was so warm, so solid, so... not a flimsy fantasy that dispersed at the first gust of wind.

I wasn't sure where that thought had come from, but it distracted me briefly from my enjoyment of the kiss.

Sean evidently could since my distraction. He lifted his head and frowned, his face only inches from mine. "What's the matter?"

"Nothing. Really."

He didn't believe me. "Are you feeling uncomfortable... about last time?" The smile in his eyes had faded into something thoughtful and sober.

"No, of course not."

"Are you sure? I know I was... intense. I hope it didn't mess things up between us."

I could suddenly see what he thought had happened. He was afraid I'd gotten scared that he'd made things too serious between us. He thought I was being skittish because of that.

And I wasn't.

Not really.

I was feeling skittish, but I didn't know why.

"I won't be that way again," he murmured. "I promise. It was just a… fluke. One bad night. I think that was the worst of it. That's not the way I really am."

Had I been feeling the way he thought I was feeling, what he'd said would have been exactly right. It would have eased my concerns about things between us jumping into intimacy, when that wasn't the way we were supposed to be together.

But that wasn't the way I was feeling.

Not really.

So his words just made my stomach twist even more.

"Ash?" he murmured, his voice thicker than before.

"Yeah."

"Tell me what's bothering you."

I would have told him had I been able to put it into easy words. But I wasn't even sure what my problem was. It was like I had this tangled mess of emotions, and they'd gotten knotted inside me so tightly that I couldn't begin to straighten them out. "It's nothing important."

"If it's holding you back, then it is important."

"I'm not holding back."

He arched his eyebrows, and that felt like a challenge. So I did the only thing left for me to do in the face of such a challenge.

I pulled his head back down into another kiss.

And that worked. I was immensely relieved when Sean stopped talking and focused on kissing me again.

The kissing lasted longer than I expected it to. He was never lax in the kissing department, but he usually got excited and moved to other parts of my body pretty quickly. Tonight, though, he didn't seem to be in a hurry, even though I could feel him growing erect against my belly.

I relaxed and enjoyed the skill of his mouth and tongue—and his hands which were doing very nice things to the parts of my body he could reach—until I felt that knot inside me start to tighten again.

Then I raised my hips to rub myself purposefully against his erection, causing him to break the kiss and groan.

After that, he moved things along. He lowered his mouth to my neck and then my breasts, teasing my nipples through the lace of my bra. Then he trailed kisses even lower—to my belly and then to the top edge of my panties.

When he flicked his tongue between my legs—just thin fabric between him and my hot arousal—I bucked up my hips involuntarily.

He made a soft growling sound. It was a new sound from him, and it made my whole body clench hard.

He chuckled, evidently pleased with this response, and gave me a soft nip through my panties.

I gasped and arched up, grabbing for his head with both hands.

His hands moved to the sides of my underwear, and I knew he was about to slide them off. Then he would move his head back between my legs. Then he would do something to me that he'd never done before.

I knew what was coming. And I wanted it desperately.

But it also made that knot of emotion inside me tighten and twist until I could barely breathe.

It wasn't rational, but it didn't matter. It was real, and I had to act on it or else do something I didn't want to do.

I tugged at his hair, and he lifted his head to meet my eyes.

I shook my head.

He drew his eyebrows together again. "Really? I was going to—"

"I know."

"You did it for me last week."

"I know. And you can do me some other time." I tried to keep my voice light, as if it were no big deal. "I'm not in the mood for it tonight."

"Okay," he said softly. "But you do want to…"

"Have sex with you? Of course I do." The naked seriousness of the conversation was making me nervous, so I pitched my voice lighter to add, "Am I crazy? You think I'd miss out on sex with Sean Doyle?"

To my relief, he didn't continue the conversation or interrogate me about my reasons. He gave me a little smile in response. He did seem more sober underneath the smile than he had before—as if some of that excitement I'd sensed in him earlier had dimmed—but he got back to business quickly. He kissed his way up my body until he'd reached my mouth again.

I felt better after that. Things felt more familiar.

He spent a while on foreplay, teasing and fondling me until I was breathless and rocking restlessly beneath him. Then he took off his bathrobe and reached for a condom on the nightstand. He'd kept my bra and panties on, and he just moved my underwear aside so he could enter me.

It felt full and familiar and deeply pleasurable, and I wrapped my legs around him in response to all those feelings. He was kissing me again as he started to move, rocking into me rhythmically, making all of me feel so good.

It felt so good.

So good.

So good.

My mind couldn't really process anything else, except how much I wanted Sean like this, kissing me, moving inside me, his bare skin pressed against mine, the heat from his body reaching me, filling me.

"Oh Ash," he rasped, breaking the kiss and tilting his head down toward my neck. His speed had started to accelerate.

I whimpered and squeezed my legs around him, meeting his motion with little thrusts of my hips.

"Ash. Baby." His was breathing fast and hard against my throat.

I hadn't been close to orgasm the moment before, but suddenly I was. It coiled inside me so quickly it was startling. I gave a ragged sob and dug my fingernails into his back.

"Yeah," he huffed, his hips working urgently. "Yeah. Come. You can come for me. Fuck, you're always so…. So good. So good. So good."

I was right on the edge now, and I was chasing it eagerly. I was riding him from below with all my strength, shamelessly taking what I needed.

And Sean was giving it to me. In his motion, in his words, in the way he'd poured himself into this one act we were sharing.

My body clamped down around his penetration as I fell over the edge.

I cried out loudly as I came—no inhibitions left, not even the ones that recognized that we were in a hotel. And Sean was right behind me, as if he'd been holding out just for me. His exclamation of release was as raw as mine, and his body jerked and shuddered as he rode it out to the end.

It took a while for us to come down, and even then we still didn't move. His body was hot and relaxed and heavy, and for some reason I wanted to feel it that way, feel how he'd taken his pleasure in me, found release in me.

But almost as soon as my body had softened deliciously, that knot in my belly tightened even more.

For the first time in the three months I'd been spending these nights with Sean, I wondered if I should have been doing it.

I hated myself for even asking the question. Sean and I had always been open and honest about what this was.

But John was who I'd always loved.

I'd been with John just over an hour ago.

And it was Sean who was panting against my neck, nuzzling my hair, pressing his weight into me, still buried inside my body.

There was something inside me that couldn't be torn in two like this.

It wasn't in my nature.

It might not have been wrong for everyone, but it was wrong for *me*.

I shifted uncomfortably until Sean finally heaved himself up and rolled off me.

I got up immediately and stretched out my hand toward me. "I'll take that if you want."

He took care of the condom and handed it to me, but his eyes were studying me closely, far more sober than he'd been before.

I escaped into the bathroom.

I sat on the toilet for a long time, rubbing my face and trying to pull myself together.

It felt like I'd made a decision.

It felt like something had ended.

Something I didn't want to end.

I still had no idea what I was going to do when I stood up, washed my hands and face, and then went back into the bedroom.

Sean had put the bathrobe back on, but he was still stretched out on the bed.

He sat up as I approached.

"You okay?" he asked, his eyes never leaving my face.

"Yeah," I told him with a smile. Until I could work things out in my own mind, I couldn't tell him anything. "I'm good."

I didn't know if he believed me when he stood up and went over to his mostly empty glass of wine. He filled it back up with the bottle, and then he gestured toward my glass, which was sitting beside it on the table.

I shook my head. "I've had enough."

He pulled his eyebrows together in that thoughtful frown I'd already seen several times this evening. "Really? You didn't even finish your glass."

"Yeah, I know. But I had a couple of drinks earlier."

The words lingered in the air for far longer than they should have.

You see, there are these moments in relationships, in regular interaction with other people, where you say certain things. And on one hand, it's just a normal thing to say, everyday conversation. But on the other, you know what you're doing in the very back of your mind.

You know what's going to happen after you say it, and you say it anyway.

Because part of you—even if it's a tiny part of yourself you prefer to believe doesn't exist—wants it to happen.

That was why I'd mentioned so casually that I'd already had a couple of drinks.

Because I wanted to say something.

Because I wanted Sean to know something.

Because I knew where this night would ultimately end, even though most of me didn't want to actually go there.

Sean had grown very still, the bottle of wine still in his hand. "When did you have drinks earlier?" he asked at last. "Didn't you come straight from work?"

"Y-yeah."

He shot me a quick look.

I gave a little shrug, feeling surreally like I was reading lines that someone else had written a long, long time ago. "I had a couple of drinks at the bar in my building after work. What's the big deal?"

"Why did you have drinks when you were coming here?" Sean still hadn't put down the wine bottle. He was gripping it so hard his knuckles had whitened.

I gave him an exasperated look. "Am I not allowed to have drinks when I want to?"

"You didn't answer my question."

"I had a couple of drinks with John," I bit out. "Is that what you wanted to know?"

Slowly—very slowly—Sean put down the bottle. "You had drinks with the jackass. Before you came here."

I made a frustrated sound. "His name is John. You know that very well."

"And you had drinks with him. After work today."

"Yes. I did."

I was starting to feel a little guilty, and it made me furious. I could acknowledge to myself that it didn't feel right for me to love John and fuck Sean at the same time. I was allowed to make that decision for myself.

Sean wasn't allowed to make it for me.

Sean wasn't allowed to have any say at all in who I loved or what I did with my body.

Sean wasn't allowed to make me feel guilty.

We weren't in a relationship.

We had a fucking contract.

I stood up and glared at him coolly. "What exactly is your problem? Am I not allowed to have drinks with who I want?"

"That's why you were late?" Sean's voice was still soft. Too soft. Unnaturally soft. As if he were reining in something powerful by nothing more than his self-control.

"I was only a few minutes late. You've been late too. So tell me exactly what your problem is." I was clenching my hands at my sides and—ridiculously—I wanted to pound on Sean's chest.

I'm a fairly even-tempered person, and I seldom lost control. I couldn't remember the last time I was so angry.

Sean said, "My problem is that every other Wednesday you're with me."

"I'm here with you."

"But you were with him earlier." His green eyes had narrowed into something hard and fierce and breathtaking. "Did you fuck him?"

I gasped. "It's absolutely no business of yours if I fuck him."

"On these Wednesday nights it is."

He meant it. He seriously believed that every other Wednesday evening was somehow sacrosanct, somehow belonged to him.

And it made me feel even angrier and even more irrationally guilty.

"No, it isn't," I snapped. "We signed a contract that states very clearly that we have absolutely no say in what the other person does outside this room. I can fuck whomever I want, whenever I want."

"So you *are* fucking him?" There was an edge to his voice that was utterly terrifying.

"You've known I was in love with John from the very beginning. You *liked* that. You *liked* that I was in no danger of falling for your irresistible self and wanting more than you could ever give me. You *liked* it. That was why you wanted to do this with me and not with someone else. So don't you dare act like I've sprung something on you or treated you unfairly."

He just glared at me, breathing heavily.

"You can't have it both ways!" I burst out, at the very end of my patience. "You can't have a casual affair at your convenience and still act all macho possessive if I spend time with someone else."

"I'm not trying to have it both ways. You can do what you want, except on every other Wednesday night. These Wednesday nights are mine."

Ridiculously, the last words and the rough texture in his voice made me shiver in primal pleasure. But I didn't let it distract me. "Nothing about me is yours."

These Wednesday nights are mine.

The words were still shuddering through me, even as I made my decision.

I released an exasperated sound in my throat at Sean's frozen figure and angry expression. Then I reached down and picked up my skirt and sweater set from the floor where we'd dropped them earlier.

I was still wearing my bra and panties, so I pulled my top on over my head and then yanked up my skirt.

"You're leaving?" Sean asked, his voice soft and rough as he watched me get dressed.

"Yes, I'm leaving. What do you expect?"

"So we have one argument and you decide this is over?"

"It's not just one argument. It's you acting completely unreasonably. It's proof that things have gotten too complicated between us to keep fucking the way we've been doing. Neither one of us wants a serious relationship with each other, so there's no reason for us to keep going through the motions." I was bending over to put on my shoes as I talked.

"Going through the motions."

For a moment it sounded like I might have hurt him, so I straightened up and gave him a quick look.

He looked nothing but tense and angry, which relieved a new sort of tension in my heart.

"So that's it?" he demanded as I smoothed down my skirt and reached for my bag.

I sighed and let go of some of my anger. "Yes. That's it. I think it's pretty clear that this is over."

As if he were responding to my release of anger, his expression relaxed slightly too. "Is that what you think?"

These Wednesday nights are mine.

"Yes, it's what I think. It's what's going to happen." I was more tired now than angry, and I was trying to hold back what felt like a loss. "I've had a good time with you. Seriously. But I think this thing has run its course."

He shook his head. "I don't think it has."

That was all it took for me to tighten with resentment again. "It's not for you to decide. I'm saying it has. I won't be here two weeks from now."

"I will." Something strange had happened to his demeanor. I'm not sure how to describe it, but it was like he'd managed to swallow up all the passion raging inside him and put it back in its place. He was almost smiling now, ironic and confident and just slightly bitter. "I'll be here, for when you change your mind."

I let out a little burst of uncontrolled sound. "I'm not going to change my mind."

"We'll see."

These Wednesday nights are mine.

I couldn't stop hearing those words in my mind.

I would have given him a proper goodbye and thanked him for the good time I'd had—for three months now—but his smug attitude was just too infuriating.

He thought he knew me.

He thought I was at his beck and call.

He thought I couldn't do without the hot sex he offered.

He was wrong.

So I didn't say anything at all as I slung the strap of my bag over my shoulder and walked out of the room.

Sean didn't follow me.

He didn't say anything.

His posture felt tense to me, but his expression was nothing but relaxed and arrogant.

And he called *John* the jackass.

I rode down the elevator feeling sick to my stomach and a little sore between my legs.

It had only been a few minutes ago when Sean had been moving inside me. We'd been as close as two people could get.

But only physically.

And that just wasn't enough for me.

I wanted love. I wanted a real relationship. I wanted a man who could give me everything, not hold back his heart because it had been wounded in the past.

Sean could never give me what I really needed.

And I was tired of settling for second best.

SIX

Two weeks later, on our regular Wednesday evening, I was resolved not to go to the hotel to meet Sean.

I'd told him last time that I wasn't going to show up, and I was determined to hold myself to that decision. I'd even taken the precaution that morning of wearing my most unattractive underwear, ones I'd never want Sean to see me in, to ensure I would stay strong.

It wasn't as easy as it should have been.

I wanted to go.

No matter how obnoxious and territorial Sean had been that one time, I had many more nights of his being smart and funny and sensitive and sexy to compare it to. I had very tangible memories of how good we were together—in bed and out of it.

Those evenings with Sean had been the most enjoyable times of my weeks, and after two weeks had passed, I was ready for another night with him, even though my mind and my heart knew it wasn't good for me.

He'd said he'd be at the hotel like normal.

He'd said I would change my mind.

I could see myself doing so. Even as I sat in my office—an hour after I normally left so I wouldn't be tempted to make a detour to a certain hotel—I could visualize myself getting up, walking the block over to the hotel, riding up the elevator, knocking at the familiar door.

Sean would tilt the corner of his mouth up with that dry amusement. Then he'd let me in and maybe make a teasing joke about how he'd been right all along.

We'd pretend the whole thing had never happened.

He would make me feel so good.

My body craved him—like an addiction. It somehow knew that every two weeks it got very special treatment from Sean, and it was expecting the same thing to happen tonight. I'd only been seeing Sean for four months. All the rhythms and pulses of my body shouldn't have transformed and shaped themselves around our nights together.

But that was how it felt.

I wanted to be in bed with him so much I could taste it.

I fought against the desire though. I wasn't going to cave. This was better for me. Prioritizing love and a real relationship, not settling for empty sex and a man who could never be who I needed him to be.

I'd miss Sean for a while. I knew I would. But I'd get over it. And hopefully I'd have a relationship with John to fill the holes Sean had left—and eventually give me so much more.

Things had been going pretty well with John. We'd been getting together a couple of times a week after work for a drink or a quick meal. I knew it wasn't really dating, but it felt like a step in the right direction.

And at least John had never acted like any part of me belonged to him.

These Wednesday nights are mine.

Tonight was one of those Wednesday nights that Sean believed were his.

He was going to be surprised and disappointed when I didn't show up.

117

I tried to be pleased by this fact, but I wasn't.

It made me feel kind of sick.

I blew out a frustrated breath and tried to focus on the contract I was writing, but the words blurred before my eyes.

I wanted to stay at least one more hour so it would be clear to Sean that I wasn't going to come.

He'd probably leave the hotel by then, so even if I messed up and accidentally made my way there, it would be too late. Sean would already be gone.

This was my plan.

Stay right here in front of my computer for another hour.

"What are you doing here so late?" The voice came from my doorway and surprised me so much I jerked.

I turned to see a smiling, handsome John Cooper leaning on my doorframe. Smiling back, I said, "Just trying to get some work done."

"Something urgent?"

"Not really."

"You want to grab something to eat?"

My heart skipped happily at the casual invitation. It was perfect. If I was having dinner with John, there would be no way for me to forsake my resolutions and go to the hotel after all. And I also wouldn't have to sit here any longer to work. "Sure. I'm getting hungry."

I shut down the computer and got my stuff together before I grabbed my bag and checked for my keys. I'd been wanting to try a new Thai place nearby and was just opening my mouth to suggest it.

"There's a good sushi place down the block," John said as we headed for the elevator.

I smiled. "Sounds good to me."

I don't actually like sushi.

I know. I know. It's an embarrassing admission. I'm just one of those people who is always off trend, no matter how hard I try to do the popular thing. It's not even the raw fish I have a problem with. It's all the crafted combinations of flavors and shapes and colors with dips and sauces I don't like and ingredients I can't recognize. It's intimidating, and I never end up enjoying it—even though everyone my age loves it.

But I didn't want to go into all that with John, who clearly wanted sushi tonight.

It would have been nice if he'd asked what I felt like eating, but he had every reason to assume I liked sushi.

Nearly everyone did but me.

We chatted about work as we walked to the restaurant, and it was crowded so we had to wait for a few minutes before a table opened up.

I scoured the menu for something that looked simple and easy to eat and felt kind of stressed when the server came over and I wasn't sure what to get.

I finally picked something out from the vegetarian section and hoped it would be decent.

If I'd gone to meet Sean at the hotel tonight, I could have had a steak.

I quickly brushed that thought from my mind.

John had been telling me—in great detail—about a client he was working with. I was happy to discuss work with him since it was something we had in common, but the story was getting a little boring.

I made myself listen, though, instead of letting my thoughts drift in inappropriate directions.

Sean's hands on my body.

Sean's lips on my skin.

Sean moving inside me.

Sean making me come.

"Don't you think so?" John asked.

I blinked, having absolutely no idea what he'd said before the question. "Oh, uh, yeah. I think so."

John nodded, so I must have responded appropriately. "Anyway," he said with a slow smile. "Enough about me. Tell me about you."

I paused with my glass of water at my lips. "What about me do you want to know?"

"Anything. Everything."

I hate prompts like that. It's just conversational laziness to give one vague question and expect the other person to encompass their whole life in a minute or two.

But people did it all the time, so there wasn't anything strange about John. At least he wanted to learn more about me. That had to be a good sign.

I opened my mouth to answer but realized I had absolutely no idea what to say. "There's nothing very exciting about me."

"I'm sure there's something."

Well, I got together with Sean Doyle every other Wednesday night for hot sex. That was kind of exciting.

Obviously, I didn't mention that detail to John.

I wasn't meeting Sean anymore anyway.

He was probably in the hotel room now, coming to the conclusion that I wasn't going to show up.

I wondered what he was thinking.

I cleared my throat. "I got As in school. I went to law school. I got this job. I work hard, and I'm always on time for appointments, and I don't even have a cat."

"Well, I for one am glad to hear that," John replied. "I'm not really a pet person."

I was a pet person. My family had always had dogs. But I worked all day, and I had a fairly long commute, so it just didn't seem fair to leave a dog by itself all day.

"That reminds me of this client I had last year." And John was off on another story, which was actually a relief since it saved me from the pressure of having to think of something to say.

Our plates came, and mine was at least edible. I didn't really enjoy it, but I didn't have to force it down.

It definitely wasn't a steak.

We ate and chatted for about an hour until John glanced at his watch and said he had to get going.

I was tired and restless and horny and a little bit hungry still.

But it was far too late to go over to the hotel even if I'd been weak enough to try.

Sean was gone by now. He wouldn't wait all night. He'd make better use of his time.

Maybe he'd go to a bar and pick up a gorgeous, sexy woman to spend the night with.

He liked having sex. It was one of the things he did to relax. He'd told me so himself.

If I wasn't providing the sex, he'd get it somewhere else.

I didn't like that idea, but I couldn't let myself think about it for long.

I couldn't be territorial or possessive. I'd gotten angry with Sean for being just that, so I couldn't be a hypocrite.

He was allowed to fuck whomever he wanted—just like I was.

And since I was no longer going to meet him on Wednesday evenings, we'd both have to find new sex partners.

John kissed me before we parted. Fully on the lips, just a little bit longer than casual.

My mind buzzed loudly as he did so.

Everything was exactly as it should be. My life was back on track.

So there was no reason for me to feel so blah and discontent and restless when I finally got home.

But I did.

~

A week and a half later, on Saturday evening, John took me out for our first real date.

A Russian ballet company was in town, and he took me to the performance.

This wasn't just a casual thing after work. This was a real date. It was significant, and it meant that my romantic daydreams were finally coming true.

I stressed about what to wear, and I stressed about how to act, and I hadn't come to any clear resolutions on either of those matters when I had to get out the door.

I was meeting John in the city so he wouldn't have to come so far to pick me up. (My apartment was in a suburb because downtown prices were too high for me.)

I had put on an outfit, but I wasn't sure it was the right one. People tended to dress up for the ballet, but how much I should dress up was a mystery. I was wearing a black skirt that flared flirtatiously at the hem and a clingy green top with a very thin cashmere sweater over it. It was kind of middle ground in possible ballet outfits, which was why I'd chosen it.

I was too stressed to enjoy the anticipation of the date, although I was relieved when I saw John wearing a black suit and with a charcoal-gray dress shirt and silver tie. My outfit seemed to match his, so at least I hadn't made a big mistake.

Once this had been sorted out in my mind, I tried to relax and focus on being in John's company. I'd spent enough time with him now that I didn't constantly feel like I was someone else in my body, but I did still feel that way some of the time.

Like when we were walking into the theater together.

The seats he'd gotten were pretty good—the first row of the balcony, right in the middle, which I preferred to being far back on the orchestra level. I had a good view of the stage and of a good portion of the other seats. I liked to people-watch in situations like this, and I had a good vantage point from my seat.

Because I was looking around just after I'd sat down, my eyes landed on one of the boxes—on our level but to the far right.

I froze when I saw who was sitting in that box.

Sean Doyle.

And beside him a gorgeous blonde with a tall, slim body. She was stunning. She looked like a model. And her outfit clearly wasn't put together from the discount racks like mine was.

He saw me too. I knew he did because our eyes met across the distance.

Maybe I should have expected it. After all, this was one of those events that rich society people often attended.

But it had never even crossed my mind that I would see Sean here—or anywhere other than that hotel room.

My stomach had dropped so dramatically at the sight of him that I was momentarily afraid I might be sick. I looked away from him quickly, focusing my eyes up on John.

John was smiling at me, saying something about how he liked these seats because they had more leg room.

I didn't give a damn about what he was saying at the moment. I was just glad I could look at him and not at Sean.

I wondered who Sean's date was.

I wondered if he was fucking her.

I wondered if he liked her better than he liked me.

I smiled and fluttered my eyelashes and put my hand on John's arm for the ten minutes before the ballet started. I knew I was playing it up more than I normally would have. I knew it was for Sean's benefit. I knew I wanted Sean to think that I was thrilled to be here with John and I'd had no second thoughts about standing him up last Wednesday night.

I knew all those feelings were rather petty and immature.

But I couldn't seem to help it.

I had to prove to Sean—and maybe to myself—that I'd made the right decision. And that he wasn't as important to me as he'd thought he'd been.

It was important that this was clear. To both of us.

John didn't seem to mind. He even put his arm around my shoulders as the lights started to go down.

I should have been thrilled by the gesture.

Instead, I kept brooding about what Sean was thinking right now and how much he was touching that blonde.

The ballet was beautiful, and I made myself pay attention to it, focusing my mind on what I was seeing and hearing instead of on the impossible man in the box across the theater from me.

At intermission I was ready for the break. Mostly because I was exhausted from making myself focus so diligently and not look over at Sean for the past hour and fifteen minutes.

I stood up, ready to stretch my legs and go to the bathroom. But John didn't want to leave our seats. He said he hated fighting the crowds. I absolutely had to use the bathroom, so I had to go one way or the other. After an extended discussion about it, I went alone to follow the slow wave of exiting people and get into the endless line for the women's restroom.

It had taken me a long time to get out of the theater, so I was very far back in the line.

I was afraid the ballet would start up again before I got into a stall.

The middle-aged woman in line in front of me was friendly, so we chatted about the ballet and why planners and architects couldn't design more stalls for women's bathrooms. After a few minutes, her husband came over to stand with her, having already used the men's room himself and then stopped at one of the stands where they were selling drinks and snacks.

He'd bought her white wine in a little plastic cup and a chocolate petit four that looked so delicious my mouth actually watered.

Her husband kept her company as the line made its slow progression forward.

I'll admit it. I was jealous. Of both the kindness of the man and the petit four.

If I got through the bathroom line in time, I was going to buy a petit four for myself.

As I waited, I glanced around, but I didn't see either Sean or his beautiful blond date.

Maybe the box seats had a private restroom or something.

I daydreamed about John showing up beside me suddenly, having braved the crowds to see if I was okay. He'd buy me a glass of wine and a petit four, and he would stay beside me the rest of the time. He would put his hand on the small of my back in that special way I'd always noticed from other men—the simple gesture that said she's with me, I'm here for her, nothing is going to touch her.

I kept daydreaming, but it never happened.

John remained in his seat, safe from the dangerous crowds.

He was probably playing on his phone while I was still waiting in line, trying not to pee in my pants.

There was an elderly lady near the end of the line. I noticed her because she was making gestures at someone across the lobby. I looked to see, and the man she was gesturing to must be her husband. He was just as old as she was, and he'd found the edge of a bench to sit on. There was a walker beside him, which he must use to walk. He and his wife were making faces at each other in a very clear silent conversation about how long the line was to use the restroom.

I kept watching them—for no good reason.

After what felt like forever, I finally made it into a stall. The lights flickered to signal the end of intermission when I was washing my hands. I hurried. I could probably make it back before the second half of the ballet started up.

No time for a petit four though.

As I was walking through the emptying second-floor lobby, I saw the woman who'd been in front of me in line. She and her husband were holding hands as they made their way back into the theater.

I don't know why I noticed it, but I did.

It made a knot in my stomach tighten.

Because I was distracted, I wasn't looking around, and so I was shocked when someone grabbed my hand and pulled me into an alcove.

Obviously, that person was Sean.

Who else would pull me into a private corner like that without warning?

I stared up at him, breathless and flushed and disoriented.

He had me pressed up against a wall, and he was gazing down at me with those lovely, clever green eyes—eyes that right now looked strangely urgent.

"What?" I demanded when I found my voice and he hadn't yet said anything.

He just kept staring at me, his body so close it was brushing against mine.

"What exactly do you want?" My voice didn't sound nearly as cool as I wanted it to be.

"You didn't show up last Wednesday," Sean murmured thickly.

I blinked. "No. I didn't. I told you I wouldn't."

"I waited for you."

My heart jumped foolishly, and I had to talk myself down by reminding myself that Sean had been waiting to have sex with me. Nothing else. "I had a good time with you, Sean. I really did. But I want more than that. You know I do."

"And you're getting it now? All your dreams are coming true?"

I had no idea how to answer that question. My dreams were coming true, but it wasn't what I'd thought it would be.

I let out a breath to relax the tension in my chest before I replied. "Whether my dreams are coming true isn't really your business, Sean."

A little light flickered in his eyes just then, as if something had made him happy. "The jackass isn't who you thought he was. You're starting to see that, aren't you?"

And that just made me mad.

I clenched my hands at my side and snapped, "And that's not your business either."

"When are you going to admit it?"

"Don't you have a gorgeous date to be getting back to?" I demanded.

His eyes seemed to caress my face, but it was fierce rather than gentle. "Are you jealous?"

Of course I was jealous.

Of course I was.

I'd had Sean every other Wednesday for four months. He'd been mine to talk to, to touch, to make me feel good.

And now he wasn't.

Now he was someone else's.

I wasn't about to admit this to him, however. I wasn't that much of a fool. "No, I'm not jealous. I have my own date. Remember? With the man I love."

I'd intended that last sentence as a kind of weapon, but there was only the smallest trace of a flicker in Sean's expression, so I didn't think the words had struck very deep.

He didn't love me.

He wasn't going to be wounded because I told him I loved someone else.

He didn't respond with words though, so I kept going. "And can I point out that this is very clearly breaking our contract? If one of us ended our arrangement, the other wasn't allowed to initiate contact afterward."

"I didn't know you were going to be here."

I believed him. "I know that. I didn't mean coming to the ballet. I meant dragging me into this corner like this."

"So you're saying you weren't going to try to find a way to talk to me tonight?"

My eyes widened dramatically. "Of course not!"

As strange as it was, this response seemed to have more effect on him than anything else. The tight urgency in his expression twisted strangely, and he exhaled in a way that made his demeanor appear to droop.

Like he was hurt or disappointed.

It confused me.

Rattled me.

Made ridiculous tears burn in my eyes.

Afraid I was going to fall apart completely, I rasped, "What exactly do you want from me, Sean? What do you want?"

If I'm being absolutely truthful, I'd have to admit that there was the tiniest part of me that wanted him to declare feelings, confess that he wanted me for more than just hot sex every other Wednesday night.

I knew better than to really believe it would happen, but a tiny, forgotten part of my heart wanted it badly.

But Sean didn't say anything at all.

Instead, he made a low sound in his throat and leaned down into a hard kiss.

The kiss surprised me. Shocked me. And so I didn't respond immediately.

But as soon as I processed that his lips were on mine, one of his hands in my hair and the other on the small of my back, his delicious heat warming me all the way to my core, then I started to kiss him back.

There was no way I could help it. Everything inside me wanted to do it.

I had to kiss him.

I *had* to.

It was more important at that moment than breathing.

I wrapped my arms around his neck and arched into him eagerly. His tongue slid into my mouth, teasing and taunting mine until they were dancing together. His hand slid down so it was cupping my bottom, and I lifted one of my legs through the slit in my skirt so I could wrap one leg around his and feel him more completely.

He was hard against me. Already. And I was throbbing with arousal too.

"Fuck, Ash," Sean muttered, dropping his head to the curve of my neck and nipping over my pulse point. "Why weren't you there on Wednesday night?"

This time the words weren't really an accusation. They were more like a plea.

I fisted my hands in the fabric of his jacket, needing to hold on to something, anything, so my whole body wouldn't fly apart.

"Fuck, I missed you," he said against my skin.

I'd missed him too. So much. And he would have to know it from my shameless response to him right now. I was practically grinding myself against him.

In public.

We were out of the line of sight of most of the lobby, and the ballet had already started, the music drifting out to where we stood.

But someone could easily see us here.

See me. With Sean Doyle. Surrendering to his advances because I craved his touch so much.

When I had a date sitting just inside the theater.

And so did he.

That thought was bitter enough to pierce through the fog of lust in my head. I released the fistfuls of his jacket I'd been clutching and flattened my hands on his shoulders to give a little push.

Barely a push at all.

He stopped though. Immediately. He didn't back up. He stood very tensely, panting loudly, his eyes closed—until he'd controlled whatever he was feeling.

Then he took a step back.

Maybe the same thought had struck him as had hit me the moment before.

We shouldn't be doing this.

I opened my mouth to say something, but there was absolutely nothing to say.

So I just walked away from him.

I walked quickly, stumbling a little since my mind and body were still spinning. I couldn't go back into the theater yet.

I was flushed and flustered and upset. So I headed toward the bathrooms.

The lobby was mostly empty now, and there wasn't a line at the restroom. I noticed the elderly man who'd been sitting on the bench was using his walker to stand up, and when I turned my head I saw why.

His wife was just coming out of the restroom. He'd waited for her the whole time, even though the ballet had started a few minutes ago.

There were tears in my eyes when I hurried into a stall, and I hugged my arms to my chest and shook for a few minutes, telling myself to get it together.

I couldn't let Sean mess up what I might have with John.

John was who I'd always wanted.

And then I couldn't help but think of one more thing.

John hadn't even come to look for me even though I'd been gone for ages now.

My throat felt full and tight still, even after I took deep breaths and then blew my nose. I left the stall and washed my hands and told myself I'd feel better about everything soon.

I left the restroom for the second time and was heading to the theater when someone stopped me again.

It was Sean, and this time he stopped me by simply saying, "Ash."

I turned around to face him, preparing for another argument.

He didn't give me one. Instead, he handed me a business card.

I noticed he was also holding something else, but my attention was caught by the card he'd handed me. It was his standard business card—the kind he must hand out to anyone he'd made professional contact with. It had his office number and business email listed. But on the top he'd scrawled another phone number.

It must be his personal number.

We weren't supposed to touch base with each other outside of Wednesday nights. That had always been one of the most important rules of our liaisons. We had never even exchanged phone numbers.

I stared at the card for several seconds until my eyes finally lifted to his face.

He looked almost sheepish as he murmured, "Let me know if you change your mind."

My lips parted slightly. I couldn't say anything.

Then Sean handed me what was in his other hand.

One of those lovely chocolate petit fours on a little napkin.

"They're really good," he murmured.

I took the tiny cake, washed with feeling so intense it shuddered through me.

Sean looked for a moment like he would say something else, but then his features twisted and he turned away.

He strode back to the box seat entrance, and I stood in the middle of the lobby like an idiot.

I did eat the petit four. It was delicious.

When I finally got back to my seat, John leaned over and said into my ear, "That must have been a long line."

~

A few hours later, John and I were at his downtown apartment.

His tongue was in my mouth, and his hand was under my top, cupping my breast over my bra. I was pushed into the corner of his couch, and he was basically on top of me.

And I didn't like it.

At all.

We'd gone to get something to eat after the ballet, and then we'd headed over to his apartment for a drink since, as he'd said, mine was too far away.

That was how we'd ended up like this.

He'd kissed me, and I wanted to be kissed by him, so I'd responded.

He didn't make me feel the way Sean did, but I tried to reason out that it wasn't fair to make the comparison.

Sean had a lot of practice in making love to me. He knew what I liked.

John didn't.

But the thing was, John didn't even try. He didn't seem to make any attempt to find out what worked for me, the ways I liked to be touched. He didn't appear to be gauging my reactions or even really paying attention to me.

He was kind of dry humping me now, his weight uncomfortable and claustrophobic.

And I swear I couldn't even tell if he knew the woman he was doing this to was *me*.

A lot of guys were like that. I knew they were. John wasn't being rough or mean or even particularly obnoxious.

He was just focused on what he was feeling and not on me.

Maybe it wasn't fair to compare John to Sean, but I simply couldn't help it. Even that first night we'd spent together, when we'd barely known each other at all, Sean had been better than this. And I understood why. He'd always recognized he was in bed with another human being and not just a life-sized doll who was there to get him off.

So as I lay against the corner of the couch with John on top of me, squeezing one of my breasts like it was a stress ball, I had to finally admit the truth to myself.

I hadn't really been in love with John for the past three years. I'd been in love with the *idea* of John I'd made up in my head. My feelings had been real, but the object of those feelings hadn't been.

Sean had been right from the very beginning. John wasn't who I thought he was.

He was nice enough and smart and handsome and a decent conversationalist, but there had been all these little details along the way that should have clued me in earlier.

There might always be little things that bug in a relationship—nobody is perfect, and expecting perfection means never finding anyone—but enough little things eventually add up to a full picture.

John wasn't who I wanted him to be.

Some men are like John—decent but selfish at heart. A lot of men are like him.

But not all men.

Some men would stand in line with their wives when they're waiting to use the restroom, they'd bring her wine and a petit four so she wouldn't miss out. Some men would wait on a bench, even after the ballet starts up again, until his wife finally comes out of the bathroom.

Some men wouldn't stay in their seats because they didn't want to fight the crowds.

And some men would know that I wasn't into this make-out session without my having to say something.

I did say something.

I put a hand on John's shoulder and pushed him away from me, murmuring, "John, wait."

He pulled away, panting. "What?"

"This isn't... this isn't working for me."

"What isn't?"

I gave a vague gesture. "This."

He frowned and straightened up. "Why not?"

Why not?

He was actually asking me why not.

"I don't know. It just isn't working."

"So what then? You want to stop?" He didn't look a bit happy about this possibility.

I hesitated. We could try it again. I could give him some direction on the kind of kissing and touching that worked for me.

But the truth was I didn't want to bother.

I knew—I *knew*—this wasn't going anywhere. So why should both of us waste any more time.

I'd already wasted three years on the man.

So I said, "Yeah. I'm sorry."

A few minutes later, I was leaving John's apartment, and I knew he wasn't going to ask me out again.

~

The next few days were bad. I spent Sunday cocooned at home, crying and watching movies and trying to reconcile myself to the fact that all my dreams had been based in thin air.

It was a real loss for me, no matter how foolish I'd been to believe in those dreams. I had to come to grips with the loss before I started to move on.

I went into work on Monday, and I didn't see John at all. I didn't know if he was avoiding me or if I was avoiding him—but it didn't really matter which it was.

On Tuesday, I was feeling more like myself, tired and sad but not about to fall apart.

And on Wednesday morning, I kept looking at Sean's business card.

I didn't have John anymore. I didn't even have the dream of John.

But I'd loved those evenings with Sean.

Even though I still wanted a real relationship, which Sean could never offer me, surely I was allowed to have some fun before I found it.

It had seemed like Sean still wanted our Wednesday nights to continue.

I brooded about it all morning as I worked.

And by lunchtime I'd finally made up my mind.

He would get to tease me and say he told me so, but I could live with that.

I was too nervous to call him, so I punched his number into my phone to send a text message.

It was only a few words.

I've changed my mind.

It knew it wouldn't last forever, but for right now second best was what I wanted.

SEVEN

I really had no idea what to expect from Sean as a response to my text message.

He'd given me his phone number, but there was no reason to assume he'd just been waiting around for me to change my mind and would want to return to our Wednesday evening agreement without hesitation. I knew very well he could find another woman—for sex or for anything he wanted—without even trying. Women must have made moves on him every single day. All he would have to do is crook his finger, and they'd come running.

He could have gotten bored or annoyed or disinterested in me—even in the few days since I saw him at the ballet.

Or he might want to make me suffer a little for dropping him the way I did.

I told myself not to expect a response very quickly—if at all—but I was so on edge after sending the text that I nearly jumped out of my chair when my phone buzzed seven minutes after I sent him the message.

It was Sean.

Tonight? Usual place and time?

That was it.

Evidently, he was ready to fall right back into our old schedule as if the interruption had never happened. That was what I wanted too.

Wasn't it?

I texted back, *See you then*, and tried to focus on work, but my mind kept straying to Sean and what would happen when I saw him tonight.

I didn't get much done all day.

~

Seven hours later, I was riding up the hotel elevator, my heart pounding painfully in my chest.

I hadn't been this nervous since the first time Sean and I had gotten together—four and a half months ago now.

Honestly, I had no idea what to expect from Sean when I entered that room, and that uncertainty was what scared me the most.

After putting on a brave face, I knocked on the door and waited until he swung the door open. Sean wore one of his regular business suits—this one a slate gray—and he wasn't smiling.

This didn't bode well for a comfortable encounter. I shifted from foot to foot and took a shaky breath.

Shit. What if he was annoyed by the whole thing? What if he didn't want to waste his time with a stupid person who'd made up a man to be the love of her life?

His face relaxed into a little smile, and I immediately felt better.

"You can say *I told you so* if you want," I said.

He stepped out of the way to let me in with a huff of amusement. "Do you really think I'm that kind of person?"

"Well, yeah. Isn't everyone?"

The hotel room was perfectly neat and utterly familiar, with nothing marring the smooth surfaces except a white box on a side table and Sean's phone lying on the table near the wine bottle and glasses. Even the smell of the room hit me with a deep sense of acquaintance. Homecoming.

It had been a full month since I'd been here, but the room hadn't changed at all.

When I glanced over, I saw that Sean was studying my face. So I added, "If the tables were turned, I'm sure I would be rubbing in the fact that you were so stupid."

"Do you want me to rub it in?" He wasn't teasing. He was asking for real.

And I grew still as I thought through the question.

Maybe I did.

Maybe I did want him to mock me for how foolish I'd been.

Maybe I thought I deserved it.

"I'm pretty embarrassed about the whole thing," I admitted.

He came closer and raised a hand to brush my hair back behind one ear. "You don't have to be. Not with me anyway."

Our gazes held for a long stretch of time until finally his face drifted toward mine. He brushed my lips lightly at first and then more firmly, his tongue darting out to trace the entrance to my mouth.

The kiss sent tingles of pleasure down my spine, but I was still too nervous to concentrate.

Sean drew back, his eyebrows lowering slightly. "Do you want to eat first tonight?"

My shoulders relaxed. "Yeah. Yeah, I do."

We both ordered steaks, and I got mine with a sweet potato (with butter, brown sugar, and pecans). Then Sean poured out the wine, and we sat down at the table to wait for our food.

"So do you want to tell me what happened?" Sean asked after we'd sipped our wine in silence for a minute.

I cleared my throat as I thought through the question. "He wasn't a total jackass."

One corner of Sean's mouth tilted up.

"He wasn't," I said. "He was decent enough."

"So why are you here with me and not with him tonight?"

"You were right about one thing. He wasn't… who I thought he was."

As soon as I'd voiced the words, my nerves seemed to dissipate. This was fine. This was comfortable. I could be honest with Sean. He wasn't judging me or laughing at me or just waiting for proof that I was an idiot.

He wasn't like that.

He was actually listening.

"So who was he then?" Sean asked, leaning back in his chair, his eyes never leaving my face.

"He was… a normal guy, I guess. Except he didn't seem to care all that much about what I wanted or even… even who I was. He asked about me but then didn't actually listen to my answers. And he'd act like he wanted to please me, but then he was mostly interested in what pleased him. He really wasn't terrible. He was never bad to me. He just wasn't… really good."

Sean didn't reply even though I paused for a break. He didn't have to. I didn't need one of those verbal affirmations to know that he was hearing me.

"I guess I'd invested him with all this thoughtfulness and sensitivity in my mind when it wasn't part of him at all." I stared down at the top of the table. "It only took me three years to find this out."

"That's not true. You didn't know him for three years. You've only really known him for a few weeks. It didn't take you that long to figure it out."

"I guess."

"I was afraid it would take you a lot longer."

My eyes lifted. "Really?"

"Yeah," he said with an ironic quirk of his mobile mouth. "I knew you'd see it eventually, but I was afraid it would take you a few months. I was imagining you dating him, living with him, engaged to him, and still not really seeing who he was."

I sucked in a sharp breath. "You thought I'd be engaged to him?"

"Why not? You were in love with your picture of him, and sometimes those pictures blind us to everything else. Why shouldn't I assume you'd follow that picture wherever it took you?"

"I'm not that stupid."

"I'm not saying you're stupid. That's my point. You don't have to be stupid to do that. Do you have any idea how many smart, generous women I've seen end up with men who don't deserve them? Because they're seeing in the man what they want to see instead of what's really there. It's not about being stupid. It's about being... hopeful."

"Hopeful." I repeated the word, thinking it through as I did.

"Yes. Hopeful."

"So why did you see what John was like from the very first minute when it took me so long to figure it out?"

Sean put down his wineglass but kept his fingers wrapped around it. "Because there's nothing hopeful about me. Not anymore."

For a moment I couldn't look away. He was telling me the unvarnished truth about himself, and it felt intimate.

Too intimate.

It made my heart clench in a dangerous way.

His phone rang then, breaking the tension between us. He glanced at it and then silenced it without hesitation.

"So what did you see in him that I didn't?" I asked, really wanting to know.

I didn't want to be foolish over a man again—not like I had been with John.

Sean gave a one-shouldered shrug. "Guys like him have had it too easy all their lives."

"Guys like him?"

"Guys who look like him."

I understood now what Sean was saying. John was incredibly handsome—and handsome in that traditional, classic way that was impossible not to notice. "So anyone who is good-looking is suspect? What about you?"

"What about me?"

"You're really good-looking." I said the words without thinking, just to make a point in the argument. After all, it was just a foundational truth about the universe—that Sean was as attractive as a man could get.

But Sean's little smile in response made me blush.

Trying to ignore the hot flush on my cheeks, I pressed on. "Don't give me that look. I'm making a point here. You're good-looking, so should I immediately suspect you?"

"I'm not good-looking the way the jackass is." I started to object, but he continued, "I'm not. I wasn't good-looking at all when I was a growing up. I was skinny and gangly and geeky, and my mouth was weird. Girls weren't into me at all until I made money."

"I... I don't believe that."

"Well, believe it. I've never had the kind of looks that open doors for you. The jackass has, and he's had them all his life. He's used to getting what he wants without even trying, and so he's never had to try to win a woman's heart."

My mind was racing as I tried to keep up with all this and piece it together into a conclusion. "So you judged him just by his looks? You're saying every handsome man is a jackass?"

"Not *every* one. But I've found a disproportionate number of them are."

I shook my head suddenly. "But *you're* good-looking. You are, Sean. You're sitting there, judging yourself."

He chuckled. "I appreciate the vote of confidence, but be honest. If you didn't know who I was, if you'd never heard me talk or interacted with me personally, if I was wearing cheap jeans and a T-shirt and you passed by me at a restaurant, you wouldn't look at me twice."

He was serious. He genuinely believed it. And I could actually understand what he was saying since so much of his attractiveness and sex appeal came from his intelligence, his sense of humor, his verbal and physical skill.

But not all of it.

"I'd notice you," I said, narrowing my eyes.

"Yeah?"

"Yes."

His mouth softened. "All right."

For some reason my heart was doing that fluttery thing again. I swallowed hard and tried to reground myself in casual conversation. "So you were a geek in high school?"

144

"Not really. I was fairly popular, but it was mostly because I made people laugh and had a lot of friends. I was smart and funny, and people liked having me around. I could always get dates, but no one was daydreaming about me."

"How do you know?"

"I know."

I'd finished my wine, and I felt a faint, pleasant buzz in my head from the alcohol. I shook my head as I looked at Sean. "You really aren't hopeful, are you?"

"No. I'm really not."

The words had a very slight poignancy to them, one that caused my heart to twist. I was saved from the trouble of answering—or working through exactly how I was feeling—by a knock on the door.

It felt like no time had passed at all, but our room service was already here.

Sean went over to let the server in, and I got excited when I saw the silver-covered plates.

When the server had left and I'd taken my first bite of my ribeye, I closed my eyes and moaned in pleasure.

"John took me to a sushi place," I said after opening my eyes to discover Sean was gazing at me with a strange intensity.

He blinked. "Did he?"

"Yes. He didn't even ask me if I liked it. I think that was my first real clue that he was mostly focused on himself." I darted a glance back at Sean's face. "Do you like sushi?"

"Sure," he said with a little shrug.

I curled up my lip, feeling ridiculously let down.

Sean laughed. "I like steak better though."

"Good."

He kept laughing to himself about this for a long time. I could see it in his face.

I was working on my sweet potato when Sean asked, "So how was the sex?"

I paused, my fork halfway to my mouth.

His question had been light and casual. Maybe too light. Too casual.

He arched his eyebrows. "Am I not supposed to ask?"

"It was…"

He leaned forward slightly, as if trying to catch the rest of my sentence.

I was blushing again and staring at my plate.

"Why don't you want to tell me?" he asked, sounding much less unconcerned now.

I lifted my head with a challenging look. "You really think you have the right to know?"

"I don't care if I have the right. I want to know." His voice was edged with something almost rough.

This was a taste of that Sean I'd seen only in the past month—in that last night we spent together and then again at the ballet. Possessive. Demanding. Something more—deeper—than the charming, casual demeanor he usually wore.

There was no good reason for me to dig in my heels about this. I could so easily admit that I'd never had sex with John, and the whole thing would go away. Sean would relax. Things would return to normal.

Fun, clever, sexy, enjoyable.

But always a little bit distanced.

Instead of giving the answer that would let us return to normal, I just took a very slow sip of wine and didn't say anything.

Sean wasn't happy about this. I could see it so clearly in his face. He was frustrated, impatient. He wanted to push me for an answer. When he took a long, deep breath, I knew he was intentionally holding himself back.

"The sex couldn't have been that good," he said at last, in a flippant tone that didn't quite match the look in his eyes. "Since you're back here with me tonight."

I couldn't think of anything to say to this, so I didn't say anything. I just kept quietly eating my steak and potato.

After a minute, Sean made a rough, frustrated sound in his throat, as if he'd lost his battle for patience.

I couldn't help but laugh. "And you were slamming John for assuming he could always get what he wanted. You can't even accept that there are a couple of things I might not want to tell you."

"That's different," he mumbled, scowling slightly.

His response was so different from his typical verbal sophistication that it excited me.

I have no idea why.

"Why is it different?"

"Because you usually tell me everything."

I started to object to this statement, but I stopped myself. Because Sean was mostly right.

I'd been more honest with him than I'd ever been with anyone—even my family, even my best friends.

Because our relationship wasn't allowed to be emotionally intimate, it had felt safe for me to open up and show him my real self.

The stakes hadn't been high enough to hold me back.

I didn't know why it felt different now, but it did.

"So the sex was pretty hot then?" He cocked one eyebrow at me, making the question almost teasing.

I couldn't help but laugh.

But I also didn't answer.

~

After we ate, Sean decided to take a shower, and I felt a wave of relief at another respite before sex.

I don't know why I wanted a few more minutes to prepare myself—since every single time I'd had sex with Sean had been incredibly good—but I did.

Tonight, for some reason, I did.

When I heard the shower turn on, I went over to the side table to look in the white box I'd noticed when I'd first arrived but then had forgotten about.

It looked like a bakery box, so it excited and intrigued me.

I lifted the lid and almost giggled when I saw what the box contained. Four beautiful cupcakes, each in a different flavor.

I was hard-pressed not to grab one and start eating, but I gently closed the lid.

Sean had brought cupcakes.

He'd never done anything like that before.

Maybe he'd thought I'd need extra creature comforts tonight, after my debacle with John.

I tried to imagine him going to a bakery and picking out the cupcakes, but then I realized he'd probably just had his assistant get them sometime today.

It didn't matter.

I was going to enjoy them.

To kill time, I walked over to look into the large framed mirror over the low dresser. I hadn't thought to brush my hair before I left work earlier, and I suddenly wondered why I hadn't freshened up a little. My hair wasn't looking smooth and shiny like normal.

I dug into my bag to find my brush, and I ran it down the length of my hair. When your hair is as straight as mine is, brushing it is really all you can do. Any hair product I tried to use—no matter how light it claimed it be—would just flatten it out. I'd washed it that morning, so it wasn't limp, but it also had almost no body.

I tried for the billionth time in my life to fluff it out, eternally hoping for a sexy, tousled look.

But no luck.

I was still staring at myself in the mirror when Sean came out of the shower, wearing nothing but a pair of black sleep pants.

The sight of him wearing those pants—which I would always associate with sex—made my whole body clench.

"What are you doing?" Sean asked, when he saw where I was standing.

I gestured to the brush, which I'd set down on the dresser top. "I was trying to do something with my hair."

He frowned and walked over to stand behind me. "Do what with your hair?"

"Make it sexy or something."

His eyes were focused on my hair, and he ran a hand gently down the length of it. "What do you mean?"

"I mean I've always wanted to have the wild, wavy, sexy hair that I see on a lot of women, and my hair has never cooperated. It's nothing but straight."

149

His expression changed, as if he were understanding what I was saying now, and he pulled my hair back in one of his hands, holding it together and then letting his fingers slide down the way I did when I was pulling it into a ponytail.

I was watching him in the mirror, so I saw when his eyes lifted to our reflection.

Our eyes met in the mirror, and that was all it took. Excitement started to pulse between my legs.

"You don't think it's sexy?" Sean murmured, taking my hair in his hand again and pulling it off my neck.

"Well... no. It can be pretty. But sexy? No." I was still watching Sean's face in the mirror, and so I saw that his gaze had turned hot, admiring.

He turned my body so I was facing the mirror directly, his body brushing against my back. Then he tilted his head down to press a kiss on the side of my neck, so softly it triggered goose bumps. "Do you really not know how sexy you are?"

I felt sexy right then. Sexy and hot and aroused. And even more so as Sean started to slide my suit jacket off over my shoulders and then dropped it on the floor at our feet.

I wore a pretty camisole-style top beneath it—ivory silk with lace edging on the wide straps. The skin of my arms and shoulders was pale and smooth, and my chest was rising and falling with my accelerating breathing. I could already see my nipples poking out eagerly, even through my bra and top.

Sean was trailing kisses along my shoulder, one of his hands curving over my hip.

I wanted to kiss him for real, so I tried to turn around, but he held me in place, facing the mirror and the dresser. "I want you to see how sexy you are," he murmured into my ear.

My breath hitched at the thick texture of his voice.

What was he going to do? Have me watch myself as we had sex right here in front of the mirror?

I realized that was exactly what he was going to do when he unzipped my skirt and let it fall down to my ankles. I stepped out of it and kicked it away.

Then Sean pulled my top over my head.

I stood there in my bra, panties, shoes, and gold necklace, my hair loose and swinging forward as my body bent slightly. I couldn't help but bend and press my bottom back against him. Everything inside me wanted to feel Sean behind me.

He pushed into me, and I could feel he was already hard in his pants. My pulse quickened, and my cheeks flushed even more.

Then Sean unhooked my bra and pulled it off. He was watching me in the mirror as he slid both hands up to cup my breasts.

My knees almost buckled.

"You are so beautiful," he said against my ear. "So sexy."

My eyes focused on his face as he released my breasts and skimmed his palms down my body until he could tuck his fingers around the sides of my panties.

I loved how intense he looked, how hungry, how feral.

I couldn't believe that expression was prompted by me.

"Don't look at me," he said. "Look at yourself."

I did as he said, and it was hotter and more vulnerable both. I hardly recognized the woman in the mirror, despite her familiar features and long red-gold hair. She was standing there almost naked with Sean's body pressed into her back, and her face was flushed, slightly damp from perspiration, and reflecting deep, sensual pleasure.

Sean pulled down my panties, and I stepped out of them. I wore nothing now except my necklace and earrings.

"There," he murmured, his hands moving back up to my breasts. "See how sexy you are?"

I closed my eyes as he teased my nipples. It felt so good I had to brace my hands on the dresser for support.

"Open your eyes. Watch yourself."

I had to do what he said. I *had* to. I don't know why it made me even hotter, even more out of control, but it did. I'd never seen myself like this before. I didn't know how to process it.

"Tell me what you want," Sean said, his mouth moving down to my shoulder again.

"I want…"

"Tell me."

"I want you to touch me."

He was touching me. He was still fondling my breasts, but I wanted him to touch me somewhere else, somewhere better. I was wet and aching, and I could feel my desire throbbing between my legs and behind my eyes.

He kept one hand on my breast but slid the other down between my legs.

I gasped when he stroked me intimately. I bent even more at the waist, holding myself up with hands flattened on the dresser top.

I'd dropped my head without thinking until Sean said, "Look up."

So I looked back in the mirror to watch myself as he fucked me with his fingers.

I was so turned on that it didn't take long. Both our eyes were fixed on my face in the mirror as my body tightened deliciously and then broke out in shudders of pleasure.

I'd never watched myself come before. I had no idea what to think.

Sean was pushing against my bottom with his erection, and I pushed back against it as my body relaxed after the orgasm.

It didn't feel like I'd had enough yet.

Not anywhere close to enough.

"Don't move," Sean murmured, stepping way and leaving me standing naked over the dresser, bracing myself, bent slightly at the waist.

He went to grab a condom and returned in less than a minute.

He stared at me for a while in the mirror without touching me. Too long. "Look at you," he breathed at last.

I was looking at myself, so I could see what he saw.

I could see how much I wanted this, wanted him. I could see how badly I wanted him to fuck me. I could see how eagerly I responded to his every touch and word.

And it made me feel sexier than I'd ever felt in my life, wanting him the way I did.

He took out his erection and rolled on the condom before he moved back into position behind me. He spread my legs apart even more and pushed on my back so I was bending more deeply. Then he started to enter me from behind.

"Keep your eyes open," he said when my eyelids automatically slid down in response to the tight penetration.

So I was looking at myself when he started to thrust.

Despite this little game he was playing, he didn't actually appear to have much stamina tonight. His rhythm was fast, urgent, and his face was already twisting with effort and pleasure.

His response just made me even hotter.

I straightened my arms and arched my back, my bottom still pressing back into him. Our flesh was slapping together as he fucked me, and it felt so good I was making little whimpering sounds.

I was close to coming again. Already.

"Look at you," he rasped, his mouth near my ear again. "Look at how hot you are, how much you want this. This is who you really are, and only I get to see it."

I couldn't help but see it too, and it pushed me over the edge unexpectedly. I gave a little sob as my body clamped down and then shook through the wave of pleasure.

He choked on a muffled exclamation as I came, but he managed to hold back his own release. He was taking me hard now, holding on to my hips to keep me in position. My breasts were bouncing shamelessly. I saw them in the mirror. My hair was swinging, and my face contorted as I felt another orgasm rising on the heels of the first.

I was almost sobbing as I came again, and this time he came with me.

I moved my eyes at the last minute so I could see his face as he came.

He looked just as needy, just as overwhelmed, just as sexy as I did.

For some reason that surprised me.

I was hot and tired and shaking and still experiencing little afterquakes of pleasure as I bent my elbows and let my upper body fall down over the dresser. I might have actually collapsed had Sean not wrapped his arms around me and then turned me around.

I propped up on the edge of the dresser for support and fell against Sean's chest. He hugged me tightly, and I wrapped both my arms and my legs around him.

I'd missed him in the past month.

I'd missed him a lot.

And I could have been wrong, but it felt a lot like he'd missed me too.

It was a few minutes before he finally released me. He kissed me softly on the mouth before he finally stepped away.

While he went to take care of the condom, I collapsed on the bed.

He returned to the bedroom and lowered himself onto the bed too, pulling me over against him.

It felt so good in his arms like this. His body was warm and relaxed now. I could feel him breathing, feel his heart beating.

I wanted to stay that way. For a really long time.

But the fact that I wanted it so much scared me, and I knew better than to invest in foolish, ungrounded daydreams again.

I'd tried that with John, and look what had happened.

I wasn't going to do it again.

So I pulled away and made myself stand up, grabbing the pajama set I'd brought with me and my underwear.

I went to the bathroom, washed my hands and face, and put my pajamas on.

I felt more like myself when I returned to the bedroom.

Sean was sitting up.

He grabbed both my hands and pulled me over so I was standing right in front of where he sat on the edge of the bed. He gazed up at me, looking like he might be about to say something significant.

My heart did a series of frantic flips.

"You feel okay about everything?" he asked.

That wasn't what I'd expected him to say. I'm not sure what I had expected, but it wasn't that.

My heart stopped flipping, and I felt a hot flash of embarrassment for thinking even for a moment he might say something else. "Yes. Of course. What do you mean?"

"You're okay with continuing this?" He gestured to the bed. "The way we were doing before. The contract and all?"

"Oh. Yes. I'm okay with it. I'm here, aren't I?"

His eyes were strangely sober as he murmured, "Yes. You're here."

He was still holding my hands, and it was making me nervous. "What's in the box?" I asked, changing the mood between us with the one question.

Sean smiled and stood up.

We ate two cupcakes—sharing them so I could taste both flavors—and we talked about work and about all the frantic plans my mother and sister were making for the wedding—which was coming up in less than a month now.

Then we had sex again on the bed, and Sean lasted longer this time.

I had a good time, and I was sated and relaxed at two in the morning when I finally left to go home.

We'd gone back to normal. In fact, we'd jumped backward to where we'd been before the anniversary of his fiancée's death, before things had become tangled emotionally.

156

It was better this way.

No confusion. No fear. No risking my heart when it wasn't safe.

I could have a good time with him and know that was all it would ever be.

I was smarter now than I'd been even a month ago.

I knew this might be only second best, but it was what I needed right now.

EIGHT

It was harder than I'd expected to wait through the next two weeks.

I was used to this schedule by now. I understood that I only got to see Sean twice a month, and I'd been living my life around that reality for months now.

Something seemed to have changed though.

I didn't know what it was, and there was certainly no reason for it. It had been very clear the last time I got together with Sean that he wanted to continue with the same rules and limitations we'd set at the beginning. We were holding with our contract.

My mind understood this very clearly.

The rest of me had trouble remembering.

I thought about him a lot. Too much. I'd wake up in the middle of the night and imagine what we'd say to each other the next time we got together. I'd wish he was sitting next to me on my couch so we could talk about the show I was watching. I wondered what he was doing at odd moments of the day. I'd take out his phone number and look at it, wishing I could just call him up.

This was stupid. This was foolish. This was something I knew wasn't good for me.

I just couldn't help it.

Maybe it was because, up until now, I'd had my feelings for John to protect me, and I no longer had that safety zone around the deepest parts of myself. I knew I couldn't have a real relationship with Sean. It wasn't only something he didn't want. It was also something he'd gone to great lengths to ensure would never happen. We had a contract that guaranteed we'd never be closer than we were right now.

There was no fairy-tale conclusion at the end of this road for me. I'd fooled myself once that a man was something other than he was, and I wasn't going to fool myself again. Not with Sean. Not with anyone.

But just because your mind knows something is true, doesn't mean the rest of you wants to believe it.

The worst part of it was that I was horny all the time.

All. The. Time.

I woke up wanting to have sex and went to bed wanting to have sex, and I gave my vibrator more of a workout than it had ever had before. Even if I could keep the emotional components of this relationship in perspective, two weeks still seemed too long to wait to have sex with Sean again.

All this to explain why I was excited and impatient and on edge as I rode up the hotel elevator on Wednesday evening two weeks later.

I was already turned on—without even having set foot in the room yet—and I didn't know how much longer I could wait.

When I got to the hallway, I knocked on the door and had to grit my teeth as I waited for endless seconds before Sean opened it.

"Finally," I said when he swung the door open to stand before me in another expensive suit.

Yes, I know that greeting wasn't very polite since Sean had taken less than a minute to respond to my knock. But it felt like I'd been waiting an eternity to get here again.

If Sean was going to be his normal cool, ironic self today and give me a lofty eyebrow arch, I was going to have no choice but to rip his clothes off.

He reached out with one hand and grabbed the front of my suit jacket, pulling me into the room and closing the door with his other hand.

"You're two minutes late," he said, a rough edge to his voice.

Then he was kissing me hard.

So I guess we were both in the same mood.

As he kissed me, he walked me over to the foot of the bed, and that was as far as we got. His mouth devoured mine, and he tugged impatiently at my clothes so he could get his hands underneath, and I fell backward onto the edge of the mattress with a little squeal of surprise.

Sean was on top of me, pushing up my skirt and parting my legs. His body was hot and heavy and hard—all of him was hard—so he'd obviously been turned on before I arrived, just like I had been.

We were so eager we hardly needed any foreplay. Sean managed to get me out of my jacket, and then he pushed my top up so he could reach my breasts. He gave one of my nipples a little bite that made me cry out as a jolt of pleasure sliced through me. Then one of his hands was in my underwear, feeling me intimately.

When he discovered I was already ready for him, he grabbed a condom and fumbled to tear it open.

As he did so, I worked on undoing his belt and trousers so I could free his erection.

So it was literally less than two minutes since I'd walked in when he was pulling my thighs apart, moving aside my panties, and edging himself inside me.

I cried out helplessly at the penetration and held on to fistfuls of the suit coat he still wore as he started to thrust.

His eyes never left my face as he took me hard and fast. He was flushed and slightly damp from perspiration, and his green eyes were hot and fierce and possessive. It felt like my head and my heart would explode. I was feeling so much. Like I'd been waiting for this for so long.

He fucked me until I came, and then he pulled out and turned me over onto my hands and knees on the bottom of the bed. We were both still wearing most of our clothes, but we still didn't have the patience to take them off. He positioned himself behind me and slid inside me again, this time from behind.

He grunted low in his throat as he started to fuck me again, and I was making sobbing sounds that were loud and helpless and would have been embarrassing in a different situation.

I lowered my head to the bedding to smother my cries as I came a second time, and then I pressed my cheek against the bed, panting desperately, when he slowed down his motion.

"You want more?" he rasped.

"Yeah. Yeah, please. I need more." I'd been waiting too long for this, and I hadn't nearly had enough yet. "I need so much more."

So he leaned forward, changing his position and bracing himself on the bed. I was still bent over with only my bottom in the air. His motion was hard and fast and almost rough, but it was exactly what I wanted to feel. The sensations spiraled up into an intense, pleasurable plateau but didn't really break, so I kept moaning and whimpering for a long time with no respite.

My body was shaking and drenched in sweat when he finally slowed down and pulled out. When there seemed to be a pause, I found the energy to look back and saw he was checking the condom.

"Is it okay?" I asked. We used condoms in addition to my birth control because we wanted to be extra careful.

"Yeah." He nodded his assurance, even as he climbed off the bed. "But we've given it a workout so I think I'll go ahead and switch it out."

My body was pulsing and felt swollen all over—not just between my legs—but I still chuckled at his dry tone. When he'd changed condoms, he turned me over onto my back and knelt between my thighs. "You still good?" he asked.

I nodded and sniffed and smiled at him, wiping some of the sweat off my face with the back of my hand. "I don't know what's gotten into me tonight, but I can't seem to get enough."

"Me either."

I was so glad to know it wasn't just me. It eased a tension in my chest, even as my heartbeat started to accelerate as he lifted my bottom to position himself at my entrance.

He held me that way as he started to fuck me again, and he seemed to enjoy the way my body shook and jiggled with his motion.

"This is what you want?" he rasped, his eyes moving from my face to where he was pumping into me.

I babbled out a repetition of *yeah* and *please*, fisting my hands in the bedding.

"This is what you need?"

"Yeah. I need it so much. So, so, so much." I hardly recognized my own voice.

"Only I can give it to you?"

Maybe at another time, I'd have had a problem with this sentiment, but at the moment it felt exactly right. Only Sean could make me feel this way. Only Sean could quench this desperate thirst. "Yeah. Only you. Only you." I cried out loudly as my body clamped down hard in pleasure. "Oh God, I need more!"

I was still wearing my shoes, and for some reason it made me feel extra-naughty. I came two more times in that position, and I was still begging for more.

But Sean had finally reached the end of his control. He'd repositioned himself one last time, bending my legs up toward my chest and then bracing himself on straightened arms above me.

I wrapped my arms around his neck, strangling on more cries of pleasure.

"That's right, baby," he said, his face just as hot and wet as mine. "Come for me one more time."

I didn't know what was happening to my body, but it was still shamelessly rocking beneath him, reaching for more satisfaction. "I need it from you," I mumbled, tossing my head helplessly. "I need it from you so bad."

"I know you do. One more time for me. Give me all of it. I want everything from you."

Either his words or his motion sent me spiraling again. My release was completely uninhibited and way too loud, but I couldn't muffle it in this position.

I was still trying to process the feelings when Sean fell out of rhythm at last. He started pushing into me with hard, jerky thrusts. He was still grunting, although louder than before. It sounded like he was saying, "Everything... Ash... everything... you're everything," with a hard push on each word.

He froze for a moment, his features contorted dramatically, as his climax hit him. Then he shook and moaned and rolled his hips as he worked through the spasms of his release.

He rolled over onto his back, and we both collapsed side by side for a long time.

I couldn't remember ever being so hot and tired and perfectly satisfied in my whole life.

I actually tried to recall another time I'd felt like this, and there was nothing.

Nothing that came close to equaling this.

When my throat finally felt like it could form words again, I turned my head to discover that Sean was looking at me.

"That was..." I panted for breath. "That was..."

"Yeah." It seemed like he knew what I was trying to say.

"I don't think I can move."

"I know I can't." His gaze still held mine, and his lips tilted up in a smile.

I smiled back.

Eventually we found the energy to get up and take care of business. We got into the shower together and helped clean each other off, but it was comforting rather than sexy. It was going to be a while before I could get the momentum of sex going again. I liked the feel of his hands stroking down my wet body though. I liked how his body felt under my palms.

He pulled me into a hug under the shower spray and held me like that for several minutes, and that felt even better.

I hadn't been careful about my hair in the shower, so it was wet when I got out. Since I didn't want it hanging like a wet mop around me all evening, I combed it out and braided it into two braids.

I look better in two than in one.

After Sean called down for room service, we both stretched out on the bed in our pajamas, and he pulled me over against him.

I was still too exhausted to do much talking, but the silence felt nice, comfortable, intimate.

When I finally shifted positions so I could look into his face, I saw he was gazing at me.

I smiled. "That was... something."

"Yeah, it was."

My cheeks were still flushed from my exertion, so I figured he couldn't tell I was blushing right now. "I've never... I mean, I've had good sex before, and it's always been good with you, but I've never... I've never been like that before."

"Yeah."

I darted my eyes up, but I couldn't tell from his expression whether he was agreeing that *I'd* never been like that before or admitting that *he'd* never been that way either. "I don't know what got into me."

"Yeah."

It would have been nice if he'd add more to the conversation than that, but Sean just wasn't the confessional type.

When I looked back at this face, his expression had changed.

"What?" I demanded.

"So you didn't have sex like that with the jackass?" His voice was light, almost teasing, but his eyes told me he really wanted to know.

I sucked in a breath. He was still thinking about the way I hadn't told him last time whether I'd actually slept with John. He hadn't let it go yet, which meant he was taking it seriously.

The truth was, I liked it. I liked that whether or not I slept with John was important with him.

Narrowing my eyes at him, I murmured, attempting to sound cool, "I thought we discussed last time that it was none of your business."

"That's what you said, but I didn't believe it." The lilt to his voice was irresistible.

I laughed. I couldn't help it. Despite my fatigue, I needed to pee again, so I hauled myself up.

But before I walked away, I looked down on Sean and said, "I'm going to give you a gift, because you gave me so many orgasms just now. Not that you deserve it, and not that it's any of your business."

He blinked.

I leaned over and kissed the corner of his mouth. Then I whispered into his ear, "I didn't have sex with the jackass."

I started to walk away, but Sean grabbed my hand and pulled me back. "You didn't?"

"No. I didn't."

He was smiling now, and the warmth in his eyes took my breath away. "Why not?"

"It's not that you've spoiled me for other men, so don't get a swelled head. I would have slept with him, but we just didn't get to that point. We only made out a few times. I figured out who he was before we got into bed."

I got up again because I did need to pee, but I could feel Sean smiling at my back as I made my way to the bathroom.

166

~

We both got steaks again that evening—I got mine with the parmesan risotto—and I greatly enjoyed my meal.

But I felt so tired afterward that I had to get back into the bed. Sean came with me. He seemed tired too.

We lay together in contented exhaustion for a long time.

I was thinking about a lot of things, and finally one of them made me speak.

I crafted my words intentionally before I voiced them. "You didn't tell me if you'd ever had sex like that before."

I made it a statement of fact rather than a question. Technically, according to our contract, I wasn't supposed to ask him about his previous sexual relationships. Of course, he wasn't supposed to ask me either, and he had no qualms about doing so.

It was only fair that he tell me something too.

When I risked a glance at him, I saw that he was studying my face soberly.

I frowned. "You didn't tell me. I told you, but you didn't tell me. Is that fair?"

"No," he admitted softly. "It's not fair."

I waited. If he didn't tell me anything right now, if he didn't open up even a little bit, the way I'd opened up with him, then I was going to have to take several steps back.

I would have no choice.

I hadn't intended this conversation to be a test, but in some ways it had turned out to be one.

Sean let out a long, slow breath, his shoulders relaxing slightly. His head was propped up on two pillows. "I've had great sex before," he said at last, the words almost hesitant. "But I can't remember it ever being... like that."

A rush of pleasure washed over me—emotional rather than physical. I didn't know what to say.

"Sometimes I feel guilty," he murmured, his eyes now focused on an empty spot in the air.

"For what?" I knew it had to do with Lara. What else would he feel guilty about?

"I wonder if I was holding back on her in some way. If I wasn't giving her everything."

I swallowed hard in the silence that followed his words.

Without question, he was holding back on *me*. He wasn't giving me anything close to everything. He wasn't even giving me a real relationship.

But he wasn't engaged to me. He'd never claimed to give me anything except sex. My situation and Lara's were entirely different, and I had no right to compare them.

I thought about his words and could understand them. It must hurt him to realize that he'd been with me sexually in a way he hadn't been with her.

"I loved her," he went on, softly, hoarsely, as if he were talking to himself. "We had a great sex life. But..."

He didn't finish the sentence. I really wanted him to, but it didn't feel right to force him.

I scooted closer to him so I could put a hand on his chest. "People are different at different stages of their lives. I don't think you can feel guilty about being a different person now than you were then. Just think of all you've lived through since then. Anyone would be different. Anyone would have grown and changed."

He turned to meet my eyes, and I saw the tightness in him soften.

I must have said the right thing.

Then his expression changed and he smiled at me. "So you didn't have sex with the jackass after all."

I gasped and gave him a swat on the chest. "I never should have told you that. Especially since you'll never tell me about your scores of sexual conquests." The words were light and teasing and intended to bring us back from the emotional precipice of the moment before.

I certainly didn't expect Sean to frown as he did in response. "What?"

I frowned back at him with a little shrug. "It was just a joke. I'm saying I *don't* expect you to talk about other women."

"You said scores of…"

I swallowed. "It was a joke, Sean."

His eyebrows were still lowered. "Do you think I'm some sort of player?"

"No," I replied quickly. "Not now. Not at all."

"But before? You think I was ever a player?"

I was about to offer an immediate rebuttal, but the words stopped in my throat. The truth was I did assume he'd gotten around—not presently and certainly not when he'd been with Lara, but he was rich, sexy, handsome, and free. It seemed obvious that he would have been with a lot of women in the past.

Sean said slowly, "I've been with nine women in my life. Is that a lot? Does that make me a player?" He was utterly serious, as if he really wanted to know what I thought about him.

I grew very still.

Nine.

It was more than me but not significantly so. I couldn't believe his number was so low.

Then I felt guilty about making assumptions based on nothing but his superficial qualities.

"I've only been with two in the past five years," Sean added very softly. "That's not a lot, is it?"

I inhaled sharply as I realized that meant Lara and me.

He hadn't used the Wednesday night contract with any other women. Just me.

It felt like my whole insides were shaking helplessly, and I had no idea what to say.

But Sean was clearly waiting for an answer.

"No," I finally managed to say. "It's not a lot."

His eyes held mine. "Are you... disappointed?"

"No," I murmured, scooting over in the bed to give him a little kiss. "I'm not disappointed."

Disappointed wasn't even close to what I was feeling.

There might have been fireworks going off in my head.

He looked like he was going to say something else, but there was a knock on the door just then.

I sat up. "What's that?"

"That's room service," Sean said, groaning slightly as he rolled off the bed.

"But our dinners already came."

"This is for after dinner."

I had no idea what it was, and I couldn't see the door from where I was sitting on the bed. So I stared in astonishment when Sean wheeled in a tray with a bottle of champagne and long-stemmed strawberries dipped in chocolate.

Sean cocked one eyebrow and looked almost sheepish. "I thought we needed to reward ourselves after our exertions earlier. Too clichéd?"

I squealed and clapped my hands with naked excitement. "It's perfect. I was hoping for dessert."

This was more than dessert, and it felt undeniably romantic as we drank the champagne and ate the strawberries together in bed.

Especially after what he'd admitted to me earlier. I was the only woman he'd been with since Lara.

But I was smarter than to fall for silly daydreams anymore.

I wasn't going down that road again.

To get myself back on the right track, I chatted to him about normal, non-intimate things—namely, work and my sister's wedding, which was coming up the weekend after next.

After I'd told him about the current crisis with the wedding flowers, Sean said lightly, "You don't seem like you're looking forward to the wedding."

"I'm not," I admitted. "I'm happy enough for my sister, but the wedding just fills me with dread. There's just so much stress involved, and all my old school friends will be there, and..."

"And what?" he prompted when I trailed off.

"And I won't even have a date." I made a face, wishing I hadn't mentioned that as soon as the words came out.

"A date?"

"Yes, a date. I'll admit it. I had all these daydreams about going with John, and all my old friends seeing me with this great guy." I shook my head. "I'm not saying I regret ending it with him. He wasn't the guy I wanted. But still... I'm not a completely insecure person. I mean, I'm proud of what

I've accomplished. I like my job, and I like myself, and I like my life. But there's always this little twinge when it comes to seeing people you used to know. You want them to... to see you doing really well. And in the case of a wedding, it means having a date."

Sean didn't appear to be laughing at me, although a smile was playing on the corners of his mouth. "So go with someone else."

"Who exactly? I'm not exactly overrun with romantic partners, you know."

"Go with anyone. It doesn't have to be someone you have romantic designs on."

"Right. So I'm just supposed to go up to my new neighbor or a random guy at work and say, *Hey, I know we barely know each other and don't take this the wrong way, but will you please go with me to a family wedding where everyone is going to assume we're a couple?*" I gave a huff of amusement.

Sean frowned. "Who's your new neighbor? Some guy you're interested in?"

"No! And would you please stay on topic. My point is that I'm not in the position to ask anyone to be my date to the wedding. What would you do if a woman approached you with that particular offer?"

"It would depend on who it was."

"Don't hedge. You know very well that I'm right. That kind of date would scare any guy off."

"It might not."

"Yes, it would." I really wasn't thinking. I was into the conversation and wanted to prove my point. "Say we didn't have a contract preventing it and I asked you to go to the wedding with me. You'd run for the hills before I could get the words out."

"No, I wouldn't."

"Yes, you would."

"No, I wouldn't. I'll go to the wedding with you if you want me to."

I stared at him. My mouth dropped open. I froze in place for several seconds. "What?" I finally forced out.

He was frowning again, like I was making a big deal out of nothing. "I said I'd go to the wedding with you. Why do you look so flabbergasted?"

"Because it's in our contract that going to social events together is against the rules."

He made an impatient face. "I'm not asking you out on a date. I'm just saying that if you need someone to go with you to the wedding, I'd go with you. What's the big deal?"

"The big deal is that people would see us there together and assume we were dating. All my friends would... They'd assume you were my boyfriend."

"What do I care about that? I assure you I'm capable of brushing off nosy questions." He sounded perfectly cool, perfectly unconcerned, as if what he was saying wasn't shaking the very foundations of my world.

"And you're kind of well known, you know," I continued, trying to even out my tone but not being very successful. "What if it ended up in the gossip columns that you were dating some nobody?"

"Are you planning to have the paparazzi at your sister's wedding?"

"No. But the story could still get out."

"They write stories all the time about me dating everyone from Queen Elizabeth to Hillary Clinton."

Despite my distraction, I couldn't help but giggle at this.

"And don't call yourself a nobody," he went on in a different tone. "I don't like that."

"I just meant—"

"I know what you meant. And I'm not saying you need to take me as your date. It's no big deal either way to me. If you want a date, I can go with you. If not, then don't worry about it."

I was still staring at him with wide eyes, but he really seemed like he meant what he said.

This wasn't an invitation to change the terms of our relationship.

He wasn't initiating a romance with me.

He was just being a nice guy.

As I thought, he kept his eyes on my face, and there was a slight tension in his shoulders that belied his casual expression.

Finally I said, "All right. If you really don't mind, it would be nice to have a date. *You* as a date."

He gave a little nod, and the tension in his shoulders relaxed. "Good then. It's the Saturday after next?"

"Yeah. It's outside the city but not far, so it should only be a few hours of your time."

"No worries."

He could say no worries. He wasn't the one who was going to attend a family wedding with Sean Doyle as her date.

I had no idea what to expect, but it made me jittery from my head to my toes.

~

We finished most of the champagne, and the alcohol made us sleepy, so we ended up falling asleep without having sex again.

At about three in the morning, I woke up in the dark room to find that Sean was practically on top of me. He was asleep, so he must have rolled over unconsciously. His body was as hot as a radiator, and he was hard in his pants.

I could feel him pressing into my belly.

I shifted beneath him uncomfortably, and my motion must have woken him up. He mumbled groggily and started to kiss me.

This seemed like a perfectly reasonable activity to me, so I kissed him back. We were both half-asleep as we fumbled together, and he ended up buried inside me. My legs and arms were wrapped around him, and I clung to him and rocked beneath him.

Sean was still mumbling, and my head was still too clouded with sleep to decipher what he was saying, but it felt soft and sweet and intimate and natural, finding each other in the dark this way.

He pumped his hips against me and buried his face in my neck, and it didn't take him very long to come.

I didn't come at all, but I loved it anyway.

We stayed tangled up together as we fell back to sleep, and I didn't want to let him go.

I didn't ever want to let him go.

I wondered if second best had ever felt like this before.

NINE

A week and a half later, as I was walking down the aisle in my bridesmaid dress, I was regretting inviting Sean.

Just a little.

Not that he'd done anything wrong. In fact, he'd done everything right. But I kept worrying that he was having a bad time or feeling awkward or that he might never want to hang out with me again.

After all, this family wedding couldn't possibly be fun for him.

I'd told him I could just meet him here since I had to arrive early as part of the wedding party. But he'd insisted on picking me up and looked a bit annoyed when I kept arguing, so I'd eventually just let it go. After we arrived, I was busy with getting dressed and helping my sister, so Sean had to sit for a long time on his own.

He was on his own for the wedding ceremony too since I had to be part of the proceedings.

What guy in the world would enjoy being dragged along and then having to sit by himself doing nothing for so long, in the middle of a bunch of strangers?

So I kept worrying—mostly about him.

The wedding was taking place outside at an orchard and farmhouse that was now hired out for events. White chairs had been placed in neat rows in front of the arbor, and I was walking down the aisle in the middle, trying to slow myself down since my habitual walking pace is fast.

I caught Sean's eye as I walked, and he gave me a little half smile, looking interested and amused and not at all bored or annoyed.

His expression made me feel better, and I had to fight not to grin at him in response.

I wished my dress were a little more attractive though.

It wasn't a terrible bridesmaid dress. I'd seen far worse many, many times. But bridesmaid dresses have to fit women of varying body shapes and coloring, so inevitably they're not perfectly flattering on everyone.

I would have gone with something less formal for an outdoor wedding at four in the afternoon, but my sister had always had visions of long, fancy dresses—for herself and for her bridesmaids. So I was wearing a satin dress with a full-length, A-line skirt, a fitted bodice, and cap sleeves.

Rose pink.

The dress was rose pink.

A very pretty color but very bad with my red hair.

But it was my sister's wedding. Not mine. She could have anything she wanted.

I hoped Sean didn't think I looked too unattractive.

The wedding ceremony itself was thankfully short—lasting not even twenty minutes—and then we processed back up the aisle and had to take all the photos.

The whole time, I was thinking about Sean, sitting alone at the reception, waiting for me to finally join him.

I vowed that if I ever got married, I was going to do the photos before the ceremony. I could live with my husband-to-be seeing me before the ceremony if it meant my poor guests didn't have to wait an hour killing time at the reception before we finally arrived.

Eventually I was able to escape and make it into the big beautifully decorated barn where all the food was set up.

It was all heavy *hors d'oeuvres* rather than plated meals, which was another relief. I looked around and didn't seen Sean in the barn, although I did notice that the tray of smoked salmon was mostly gone since we had taken so long with the pictures and that also there were no more chocolate-dipped strawberries.

Typical.

Cursing the extended photo session, I wandered outside to the patio where little tables had been set up for guests to sit.

I found Sean at a table in the corner under the shade of a tree. He'd managed to snag the best seat.

That too was typical.

"Sorry," I said, sitting down at the empty chair next to him. "Sorry it took so long."

"That's the way it always goes when pictures are afterward." He looked relaxed and like he was in a good mood, so he must not have gotten too impatient waiting.

He slid a plate over to me, on which was a very good variety of the best food, including smoked salmon and dipped strawberries.

I stared down the plate speechlessly.

"It was going quickly," he explained, as if responding to my expression. "So I went to get you some."

I lifted my eyes to his face and whispered, "Thank you."

His eyebrows lowered. "You okay?"

I shook off my strange reaction. "Yeah. Sorry. It's just the whole thing has been pretty stressful, and it all took so long, and you've been waiting here for ages…"

"Don't worry about me. I've been fine. I know how weddings go."

"Have people been staring at you?"

He chuckled. "A few."

"They recognized you, I guess."

"Yeah. At least some of them did. One old man came over and pitched me a real estate deal."

I'd been munching on my food, but at this my mouth almost fell open. "You're kidding! Who was that?"

Sean nodded over toward an elderly man dozing on a bench by himself.

I giggled. "That's my great-uncle Larry. I can just imagine his pitch." I peered at Sean's face but saw nothing except amusement, so he really must have meant it when he said he wasn't bored or annoyed.

"It was something. Then he got angry because I said I wasn't sure it would work out for me, and he snapped that he expected more from Ashley's fella."

I paused, a cracker halfway to my mouth. "Sorry. I told you that's what everyone would think if you came with me."

"Stop saying sorry," Sean said, standing up with his empty champagne glass. "I can think of worse things than being called your fella."

I couldn't think of a response to that, so I just sat there, my mind whirling, and watched Sean walk over to get more champagne and also a glass for me.

He brought them over, and I accepted mine gratefully.

I really wished I knew what Sean was thinking, but his face was as composed and clever and unreadable as ever.

~

The reception was the best part of the wedding, as far as I was concerned.

We did have to put up with curious people coming over and asking needling questions of us, but Sean was clearly a master at that sort of thing and managed to end the interrogations before they really started, without ever seeming rude. He always just changed the subject without the other person realizing what was happening.

My sister and her new husband came over, but my sister was in too much of a tizzy to really focus enough to be curious about Sean and me. I told her we'd met because we both worked in real estate, and that seemed to satisfy her.

When my mother came over, it was more awkward since she kept talking like Sean and I were a couple. I tried to gently set her straight, but I wasn't sure she got it.

That meant I'd have some work to do with her after this was over so she wouldn't start planning *my* wedding.

But all in all, it wasn't as uncomfortable as I'd feared, and Sean didn't even appear in a hurry to leave.

When the cake was cut, he made a point of getting a piece of the wedding cake to save for his grandmother. He said he always saved her a piece whenever he attended weddings. It was some sort of tradition they'd had since he'd been a kid.

I thought it was kind of sweet.

When all the other traditions were completed, my sister and her husband did their first dance on the part of the patio set off as a dance floor. Then she tried to get other people to dance too.

No one really wanted to.

Some settings lend themselves to dancing, and some do not. This was an outdoor wedding in the afternoon, and it was now just after six o'clock. It was getting a little chilly, and everyone had eaten a lot. No one wanted to get up and look stupid on a makeshift dance floor.

I shook my head. "She's always had these daydreams about one of those big festive occasions where people stay and dance through the night. Sort of like those big parties in *Sabrina*."

Sean must be familiar with the movie because he nodded. "It never turns out that way, does it?"

"Nope." I sighed when I saw my sister gesturing toward me urgently. "Shit. She wants me to dance."

Sean chuckled. "Well, you better be a good sister then." He stood up and extended a hand toward me.

I took his hand as I rose, but I stood still as I murmured, "You don't mind?"

"What? Doing a cheesy dance with you at a wedding reception? I think I can tough it out."

So Sean and I walked to the dance floor. He was still holding my hand. An over-the-top rock ballad was playing through the speakers—one of my sister's favorite songs as a teenager—and Sean put his arms around me and pulled me toward him.

I'd never been much of a dancer, but it really didn't matter in this context. Sean got us moving to the right rhythm, and the song was slow enough that we could just sort of rock together.

I'd have enjoyed it more if everyone hadn't been staring at us, but I did like the look in Sean's eyes. Amused. Teasing. But also almost... fond.

He seemed to be enjoying himself as much as anyone could in such a situation.

I wasn't going to fool myself though. Not again.

Sean might have been the perfect date to my sister's wedding, but that didn't mean we're anything more to each other than we'd ever been.

We still had a contract.

After today was over, we were likely to go right back to where we'd been before.

Meeting every other Wednesday night.

Nothing more.

I was wanting more. No point in denying it. But that look in Sean's eyes wasn't a promise of a future.

It was just Sean Doyle being himself.

~

I was quiet on the way home.

It was dark by the time we were finally able to leave, and I was exhausted. I also felt a bit rattled, and it worried me. I didn't want my emotions to be confused where Sean was concerned. It was simply too dangerous. But I wasn't sure how to help it.

We had to drive almost an hour to get back to the city, and my place was in a suburb on the other side. I'd changed into leggings and a long top, so I was comfortable physically.

But only physically.

I felt bad about Sean having to drive so far, but he was the one who'd insisted.

We were approaching the city when Sean murmured into the silence, "You okay?"

I straightened up and looked over at him in the dim light of the dashboard. His eyes had been on me, but now they turned back to the road. "Yeah. Yeah, I'm fine. Just a little tired."

"You're quiet."

I was quiet. I knew I was. "Yeah."

"Anything you want to tell me?"

I sucked in a breath. "What do you mean?"

"About why you're quiet," he explained, his voice as soft as before.

I had no idea what he was getting at, but I wasn't about to tell him how I was feeling. Soft and confused and excited and a lot of other things that would be mortifying to admit.

So instead of telling him the truth, I said lightly, "I think it's just the letdown. After months of stress and planning over the wedding, it's finally over. You know what I mean?"

Something flickered briefly on his face—something akin to disappointment—but it was gone before I could register it or read it accurately. "Yeah. I know what you mean." He cleared his throat. "Do you mind if we make a stop on the way to your apartment?"

"Sure. Where did you want to go?"

"My grandmother's. I wanted to give her the piece of cake. It's right on the way."

"Of course. No problem at all."

Now I was even more flustered. Surely he didn't mean he was going to take me in to meet his grandmother. That would be... unbelievable.

Maybe he was just going to have me wait in the car while he ran in to give her the cake.

That would be fine.

That would be no problem.

That wouldn't make me feel like my head was about to explode.

Sean had been telling the truth. His grandmother lived in an established neighborhood of old row houses in what once would have been the edge of the city, before Boston had grown up past it. It wasn't much out of our way, and it didn't take very long to get there at this time on a Saturday night.

He parked the car in the narrow driveway and unbuckled his seat belt to reach back and get the little box in which he'd put the cake. He drove an expensive dark blue SUV, far nicer than anything I'd ridden in before.

When I just sat there, he frowned at me. "Are you coming?"

My heart jumped into my throat. "Uh. Yeah."

I guess he was expecting me to come inside after all.

~

Sean's grandmother was a tiny woman with salt-and-pepper hair. Her accent wasn't quite as exaggerated as the Irish brogue Sean had used when he was describing her to me, but it was close.

She was wearing a heavy bathrobe that zipped up the front, but she'd obviously not been asleep because the television in the kitchen was blaring.

She appeared delighted to see us as she hugged and kissed Sean and then hugged and kissed me.

She kept up a nonstop running commentary as she told us to come in and split the piece of wedding cake with a cup of tea.

When we went into the warm kitchen with a big table crowded into one corner, she muted the television and put water in the kettle.

"So you're Ashley," she said with a smile at me.

My shoulders stiffened, and I darted a look over at Sean, but he wasn't looking in my direction, and there was no way to tell from his face whether this was just something his grandmother said or if she'd actually heard my name before in conversation with her grandson.

Surely he wouldn't have told her that he got together with me every other Wednesday for sex.

That wasn't appropriate grandmother conversation.

"Tell me about your people," she said, pulling mugs off a shelf above the counter. "With that lovely red hair, you must have some good roots."

Good roots to her probably meant having Irish in the family. Since I did, I explained to her that my grandfather on my father's side came from an Irish family, but the rest of me was German and French.

I was afraid she might be disappointed in my watered-down bloodline, but she just smiled and nodded in interest.

She poured hot water into the mugs and brought them over to the table with a box of tea and the cream and sugar. I started to take care of my own cup, but Sean put a hand on my knee under the table.

Meeting my eyes, he gave the slightest gesture of his head toward his grandmother, clearly indicating that she was supposed to prepare the tea herself.

She fixed our tea, asking if I wanted cream and sugar in a tone that made it clear she expected me to drink it like that. I said yes, of course, and happily drank what she prepared for me.

Then she cut the small square of wedding cake into three pieces and passed them around.

"So Sean always brings you wedding cake?" I asked when the conversation had hit a lull.

"Oh yes, he does. Ever since he was thirteen years old."

Sean was smiling at his grandmother, but I thought he looked just slightly tense. I wondered why.

"How did that start? I asked, genuinely curious.

"When he was thirteen, he had to go to a second cousin's wedding, and he was in a kerfuffle about it."

"I wasn't in a kerfuffle," Sean muttered dryly.

"Yes, you were. You didn't want to go. You thought it would be dumb and boring and you'd be the only boy your age there. You'd been told you'd have to dance with a pretty little cousin, and you were dreading it. You complained about it for weeks. You were in a kerfuffle." She gave her grandson a chiding look as she spoke.

Sean let out a huff of amusement. "All right. I was in a kerfuffle."

"I'd broken a hip, so I wasn't going to be able to go. So I told him he was responsible for bringing me a piece of wedding cake. That gave him a mission, see?" She patted Sean's hand fondly. "Sean has always needed a mission to feel comfortable."

Intrigued by this, I studied his face. He was staring down at his teacup, not looking at me at all. I thought he appeared a bit self-conscious, although I'd almost never seen Sean look that way before. "A mission?"

"Yes, a mission. Something to accomplish. A structure and purpose to the way he approaches the world. Otherwise, he gets very upset by all the different things he feels."

"Grandmother," he muttered under his breath, slanting her a look.

The old lady was completely unaffected by the warning in his expression. She laughed and reached over to pat his hand on the table. "Don't be embarrassed by it, boy. You feel very deeply. You always have. There's nothing wrong with feeling a lot and occasionally being scared because of it."

For some reason I was feeling a lot too, and it had something to do with seeing Sean in this new context. He wasn't the master of the room here. He wasn't completely confident and in control.

He was a grandson. A regular person.

Not all that different from me.

"Ever since that wedding, he's always brought me a piece of cake. He's never forgotten his old grandmother." She smiled at Sean affectionately. "He's a good boy."

"I'm thirty-eight years old now, you know," Sean murmured. He didn't sound bad-tempered, but he did sound a little stiff.

"What does that have to do with anything?" His grandmother turned to give me a very speaking look. "He's a good boy. He never forgets me, no matter how big he's gotten to the rest of the world. He doesn't always know how to talk about it, but he does know how to love."

I froze, my mug halfway up to my lips.

For a moment I literally couldn't move.

It felt so much like she was trying to tell me something, but it couldn't be what I was thinking.

Surely she couldn't think that Sean...

Surely she wasn't assuming that he...

Maybe she *was* assuming that. After all, he'd brought me in to meet her. She wouldn't know that our relationship was bound on all sides by an ironclad contract Sean had no interest in revoking.

I wasn't going to be an idiot.

Not twice in one year.

It was so easy—too easy—to read what you wanted into a relationship, into what felt like clues and undercurrents that were all pointing the way you wanted them to. And then you ended up with a broken heart or broken pride or both.

I'd done it with John. I wasn't going to do it again.

"Okay," Sean said, firm authority in his tone that broke through my muddled thoughts. "We should probably get going."

I didn't really want to leave. I wanted to hear more about what his grandmother had to say about Sean.

But she was getting up and pulling Sean into a big hug, so it was clear our time here was over.

His grandmother said something into Sean's ear after she hugged him, but I couldn't hear what it was.

As we were walking back to the car, Sean murmured dryly, "Sorry about that."

"Sorry about what?" I asked, pleased that my voice was composed and natural. "That your grandmother acted like a grandmother? You don't have to apologize for that. You put up with my family today, so it's only right that I reciprocate. Anyway, I liked her."

Sean's shoulders relaxed, and he smiled at me, so I must have said the right thing.

~

When we got to my apartment complex, a car was backing out of one of the few guest spots, so Sean waited for the other car

188

to pull out and then took the space. Without speaking, he got out of the car and walked me to my door.

I had my keys in my hand as I turned to face him, feeling shy and a bit uncertain. "Thanks for coming with me today."

The corners of his mouth twitched up. "Of course."

He stood about eight inches from me, and I wondered what he was thinking. His eyes had taken on a certain heat that I recognized very well, but there was more in his expression, more that felt too deep, too complex.

Not nearly as simple as lust.

I asked, "Do you... do you want to come in?"

"Do you want me to?" He was studying my face now, like he was trying to read my expression in the same way I was trying to read his.

"Y-yes."

He must have heard my slight hesitation because he didn't move. "We can just meet on Wednesday like normal, if you'd rather."

I shook my head. "No. I do want you to come in. It just seems... different. Since this isn't a hotel."

"No," he said, leaning forward and brushing his lips against mine before pulling back. "It isn't."

The kiss was all it took for me to decide what I wanted.

Of course I wanted *him*.

I reached out for him as soon as he'd pulled away, and I'm really not sure of the exact steps that happened after that. I must have unlocked my front door, and we must have gone inside my small one-bedroom apartment (which was fortunately neat since I'd straightened up a little that morning). We must have made our way to my bedroom and then taken off our clothes. And we must have lowered ourselves onto the bed.

I don't remember doing any of that. Emotion and need and knowledge had exploded in my heart, in my mind, leaving a thick cloud of desire and feeling that blurred all the edges, blurred everything except him.

Sean. Kissing me. Touching me. Being with me.

Being Sean.

In my home and not some impersonal hotel room.

Before I knew what was happening—or how it had happened—we were under the sheets together, kissing and moving against each other, both of us completely naked.

With my nightstand and little brass lamp to the right of us and my favorite painting hanging on the opposite wall.

This was me. Fully me.

And I wasn't with a pale, fluffy fantasy of a man. I was with Sean Doyle.

The real Sean Doyle. A real, living, breathing man. With family and wounds and insecurities and needs.

My heart was racing from far more than desire as he kissed his way down my body.

I was terrified as much as I was yearning for him.

We hadn't turned on the bedroom lights, but light came flooding in from the hallway. I could see his face clearly when I lifted my head from the pillow and saw him raise his head from my belly.

He was panting as fast as I was, and his hair was slightly mussed. We held the gaze across my body.

Then he asked in a soft, hoarse voice, "Can I do you tonight?"

The words were vague and not particularly sophisticated. They felt raw, naked, rather than sexy.

I knew what he was asking. I'd never let him go down on me before.

And he wanted to. He wanted to please me that way. Even though I could feel the hard tension of arousal all through his body.

I heard myself saying, "Yes, please," before another part of my mind could rear up in fear. His expression changed, softened, at my response, and he leaned down to press a soft kiss just below my belly button.

Then he kissed his way down.

I squirmed slightly, my arousal throbbing as his mouth got closer and closer. I didn't understand why I felt so completely vulnerable, but I did. I was shaking slightly as he nuzzled between my legs.

"Sean." I gasped, clutching at his hair. My legs were wide apart, bent up at the knees. He'd parted my outer lips and extended his tongue to give me a quick lick.

He glanced up again at my face. I can only imagine how I must have looked. But there was that same heat in his eyes that was made up of so much more than lust—possessiveness and need and affection and other things.

So many other things.

"Ash," he murmured, his eyes holding mine. "Let me make you feel good."

I nodded, my fingers tightening in his hair as he lowered his face again. I couldn't speak, and I couldn't hold my hips still, and I made a wordless sound of pleasure when his tongue got going again.

He'd always been good with his mouth, and there was no exception with this activity. He teased and played until I was whimpering helplessly, and then he slid two fingers inside me, curling them up, and he gave my clit more focused attention.

I'd hooked my legs over his shoulders, having to fight not to squeeze his head between my thighs, and I was still grabbing at his head, his hair, rocking my hips shamelessly into his mouth.

I could feel my orgasm rising, but it wasn't coming in one of those quick flashes. It was slower, deeper. I knew it was going to be good, and it felt totally out of my control.

Sean was making little sounds in his throat as he worked, and I knew he was enjoying my responsiveness, my complete lack of inhibitions. He had a handful of my bottom, holding me in place. With his other hand, he was still fucking me with his fingers, and then he started to suck hard on my clit.

All the tension in my body suddenly shattered, and nothing could contain my loud cry of pleasure as I rode out the orgasm against his fingers and mouth. My channel was squeezing hard around his fingers, and he pushed against the spasms. My clit was so sensitized it almost hurt as he gave it a few last flicks with his tongue.

I was boneless and gasping when he finally lowered my body and straightened up. His fingers and his mouth were both wet, proof of how much I'd enjoyed what he'd done to me.

For me.

I shook helplessly in the aftermath, naked on the bed, until Sean wiped his face with the back of his hand and moved up over me again.

I thought he would kiss me, but he didn't. Instead, he pulled me into a hug. I clung to him, needing his strength and support as much as I'd needed the orgasm earlier.

"You okay?" he murmured into my ear after a few minutes. He was still aroused. I could feel his erection against my body.

"Yeah." I took a deep breath and released it. "I'm good. That was... amazing. Thank you."

He lifted his head and wiped away one little tear that had leaked out of my eye. I hadn't even been aware of it. Then he leaned down to kiss me. "You're welcome, baby," he murmured against my mouth.

I wrapped my arms around him and kissed him back, and soon he was rocking his erection against me. We had to briefly separate so I could find a condom in my nightstand drawer and put it on him, but then we were kissing again, and he was easing himself inside me.

It felt so good, so familiar, and so new at the same time. Since this was my bed, my room, my home.

"Wrap your legs around me, baby," he said, gazing down at my face as he gave a little thrust.

I did as he said, loving how it changed the angle of penetration and got him even closer to me. I pulled his head down so I could kiss him again as we started to move together.

It went on for a long time, just kissing and rocking together, and every part of it felt so good that my mind could barely process it.

I couldn't stop. Kissing him. Holding him with my arms and my legs. Lifting my hips to meet his thrusts.

"That's right," Sean rasped, breaking the kiss at last as his motion grew faster. "I can feel you getting tighter. Can you come again?"

"Yeah, yeah, yeah." I huffed out the words on each taken breath. My fingers were now digging into the skin of his back.

Sean was staring down at me as I tossed my head restlessly with the rising of my climax. "I want to feel you come. I want you to let go. Don't hold anything back. Not from me. I want everything from you."

His words as much as his motion pushed me over the edge, and I arched up, my mouth opened with a silent scream as the sensations pulsed through me.

He groaned as my body clamped down around him, but he managed to hold on to his fast, steady rhythm.

I squeezed my legs around him as I came down from my orgasm. I tightened my fingers in his hair.

Sean was panting now, his features twisting as he was reaching the edge himself. "That's right, baby. Hold on to me. Don't let me go. This is... this is what I want."

I didn't know if he was even aware of what he was saying, but the words sent my heart into a tailspin. I was almost sobbing as he fell over the edge, as I watched his face transform with pleasure, with satisfaction, as his body shook helplessly, as he jerked against me with a series of hard pushes.

We were both groaning and panting as he collapsed into my arms afterward. His body was hot and relaxed and heavy, and I didn't want to let him go, even though my legs were stiff, even though I knew he needed to take care of the condom.

I finally lowered my legs reluctantly as he pulled off me.

I could barely move, so I just stayed where I was, naked on the bed, as he got up to throw away the condom.

He returned to the bed without a word, moving beside me and then taking me into his arms.

I breathed against his chest, listening to his fast heartbeat.

My heart was beating quickly too.

Sean stroked my hair.

I pressed a few kisses against his shoulder.

Neither of us said anything.

Eventually I fell asleep.

~

I woke up when Sean was trying to get out of my bed.

I'd slept hard—really hard. I hadn't moved or woken up at all until I was vaguely aware of Sean trying to move me off him. I didn't want him to get up. My body really liked how it felt to sleep against him. So I clung to him, resisting the change in position.

I was vaguely aware that Sean made a strange sound, and I woke up as I tried to figure out what it was.

"Sorry," I mumbled as I realized what I was doing. I was clutching at him, trying to keep him from getting up. I rolled onto my back and relaxed my arms. "Sorry."

"It's fine," Sean said. He straightened up so he was sitting on the edge of the bed. I could hear him breathing deeply, but I couldn't think clearly enough yet to figure out what he was doing.

I turned on my side and tried to see his face. He seemed to be staring down at the floor.

Then I looked at the clock and discovered it was three-thirty in the morning.

It was a Sunday morning. The bed was so comfortable. It would be even more comfortable with Sean in it. "You can stay," I said. "You don't have to leave yet."

He didn't move, except for his head, which turned to dart a glance at me.

"Unless you want," I added, suddenly feeling terrified for no good reason.

He didn't reply with words. For a while he didn't even move. Then he stood up with a soft groan and went into my bathroom, closing the door behind him.

While he was in there, I woke up completely. I got up to find a big T-shirt and a pair of panties to pull on since I'd been sleeping completely naked. Then I sat on the bed and waited for Sean to return.

When he did, he didn't get back into the bed. He reached down for his underwear and trousers on the floor.

He was going to leave.

I don't know why it bothered me, but it did.

A knot clenched in my gut that got tighter and tighter as I watched him dress in silence.

Surely there wasn't anything he had to do first thing on a Sunday morning.

He just wanted to leave.

Of course he did.

Why wouldn't he?

We'd never been in a relationship.

We just met every other Wednesday for sex.

Yesterday had been an aberration, but it hadn't changed our situation.

Sean was leaving.

He was a really good guy at heart, but he didn't want anything but sex from me. He might like me—I knew he did—and occasionally he let even more feeling leak through the edges of his behavior.

But he'd never let himself feel anything more. Even if he was tempted, he would stop himself so his heart would never get ripped out of his chest again.

Every day, he made conscious choices not to change his mind.

Something had changed for me though. I knew now that I wanted so much more.

I wanted everything.

Not just in theory. Not in some flimsy daydream.

I wanted everything from Sean.

When he was dressed, Sean leaned over to give me a kiss. "See you on Wednesday night?" he asked lightly.

The casual question was like the stab of a knife in my heart.

It wasn't his fault. It was mine. He was being who he'd always been, assuming nothing was different.

When everything was different for me.

I wanted Sean badly but not enough to damage myself trying to keep even the little parts of him I currently possessed. I knew exactly what I needed to do.

If he wasn't going to let himself love me, then I couldn't hurt myself making do with the little he would give me.

"I... I don't think so," I said.

I saw Sean's body jerk slightly. He was silent for a beat. Then asked, very softly, "You won't be there?"

"No."

"Why not?"

Despite the clause in our contract that claimed we didn't owe each other an explanation for ending our affair, I knew I did owe Sean an explanation.

I just wasn't sure what I should say.

I took a ragged breath and shifted slightly from where I was sitting on the bed. "It's… It's just not enough for me anymore. I know I was totally wrong about John. I know I was stupid. But I still think that what I wanted from him—what I wanted from a relationship—was valid. I want someone to love me. I want someone to love. And what I have with you is… is great. It's really… great. But it's not love."

I don't remember ever baring my soul so completely to another person. The words stripped me bare and hung in the air for a long time after I spoke them.

I knew what I wanted to happen.

I wanted Sean to come over and take my hands in his. I wanted him to kneel down and admit that he did love me, that he wanted me to love him. I wanted him to say the Wednesday night meetings weren't nearly enough for him either.

I wanted him to want everything too.

It was a long shot. Obviously. But after what had happened between us the night before, I thought it could be possible.

He'd seemed to be feeling more for me than just lust and companionship.

Or maybe I was just imagining it. Making it up in my head—like I'd always done before.

Because Sean didn't come any closer. And he didn't reach out to take my hand or touch me in any way.

He stared at me for a long time. Then he finally murmured, "All right. I understand."

It was the worst thing he could have possibly said to me, proof that he didn't even feel enough for me to argue, to get upset.

He was just going to let me go.

I pulled one of my knees to my chest and hugged it. I had to swallow a few times before I could speak through the lump in my throat. "Okay. Thanks. I... I've loved the time we spent together."

It was the closest I could come to telling him that I loved him.

Because I did.

I loved Sean Doyle.

More than I'd ever loved another man in my whole life.

"Me too," Sean murmured, his voice just slightly thick. He leaned over again and gave me one more, very light kiss.

Then he was leaving.

Walking out of my life.

Walking out of my life for good.

It didn't feel right.

It wasn't the way the universe should have turned.

But there wasn't anything I could do to stop it.

I'd known from the beginning that Sean had loved a woman once, and he was never going to let himself do it again.

In a different world, he and I could have been happy together.

But that wasn't this world.

In this world, he was who he was.

When I heard my front door close, I curled up in my bed and cried.

It was terrible. Absolutely terrible. To lose Sean the way I had.

But even in my grief, I knew I'd done the right thing.

Sean would never be second best to me. Not anymore.

And it would be a lie—an absolute lie, to him, to myself, and to the world—if I continued to act like he was.

TEN

I'd been crying in my bed for about five minutes, and I had no plans to stop anytime soon.

Then part of my mind became aware of a noise in my apartment. I couldn't think clearly enough to place it before I saw the silhouette of a man in my bedroom doorway, standing against the light of the hall.

I squealed and sat up, my fight-or-flight instinct kicking in before I realized the man was Sean.

He must not have locked the door on his way out, so he'd been able to walk back in.

"I'm sorry," he said, his voice sounding very rough, very strange. He strode across the room and took both my hands in his. "I'm sorry. I just came back in. I wasn't thinking I'd scare you."

"You did!" I gasped. "What are you doing? I thought you'd left."

"I had," he said, still sounding so strange. His face was twisted with what looked like emotion. I'd never seen him like that before. He was always, always so controlled, so self-contained. He knelt down on the floor in front of me, still holding my hands in his. "But it was wrong. It was all wrong."

"It wasn't—"

"I know it wasn't wrong for you," he interrupted. "It was wrong for *me*. I shouldn't have left. It was wrong. I know you want more, and I know you think you'll never get more from me—but I really..." His voice seemed to run out, and he swallowed, cleared his throat, and tried again. His face was damp with perspiration, and his eyes were nakedly emotional.

"I really think I can give you what you want and need. I think I can if you'll give me one more chance."

I was frozen, breathless, staring at him blurrily. My mind simply couldn't keep up with what I was hearing.

This wasn't really happening.

It couldn't be.

It had to be part of a desperate, needy dream I'd concocted through my heartbreak.

He didn't seem to mind that I hadn't said anything. His words kept spilling out in a clumsy overflow so uncharacteristic of his usual articulateness. "You were right about everything you ever said about me. I thought up this Wednesday evening plan on purpose to protect myself. I liked what I saw in you from the very beginning. I liked it so much it scared me. I had to protect myself so I wouldn't fall again, so I wouldn't be hurt like I'd been hurt before. You were right, and I was selfish. Selfish and—"

"I never said you were selfish!" I don't know why this was the detail that finally pushed me into speech, but it was.

"I know, but you meant it. I know you did. And I *was*. I was selfish and scared and tried to arrange this whole thing to suit my needs, without ever thinking... See, you were in love with the jackass, and I thought it would be safe. You have no idea how much I hated him. Oh how I hated that man. It hurt so much when you started to date him, and then you stopped seeing me, and I knew I hadn't protected myself the way I'd tried, but I thought it was too late."

He stopped, taking a few ragged breaths and staring down at my hands in his.

Mine were trembling. There was no way I could make them stop. My throat hurt, and my eyes burned, and it felt like the whole world was starting to crumble at the edges, like it would cause a landslide I'd be buried beneath forever.

Sean raised his eyes to mine again, and I still couldn't believe what I was seeing in them, something out of my most over-the-top daydreams. "Then you dumped him and wanted to start again, and I was... I was terrified. My grandmother is right about me, you know. She said that I only feel comfortable if I have a mission, a structure and a purpose to channel all my feelings into. That's why I had to hold on to our contract and our Wednesday nights. It was the only thing making me feel safe. But again, I was just thinking about myself. Not you. Of course you need more. I should have offered you more from the very beginning. That very first night, when I followed you into that bar, I should have asked you out on a real date. Because I... I liked what I saw in you so much."

I was gaping at him now. Literally gaping. I would have been embarrassed by my reaction had my heart not been exploding with something else. I tried to say something but couldn't.

Sean didn't appear to expect me to talk. He was still rambling on like he couldn't stop. "I didn't mean to fall in love with you. I was... I thought I could do it. I thought I could keep you at a distance where it was safe. But I couldn't, and I did fall in love, and then I didn't know what to do. So I guess I was trying to change things between us without actually doing it—taking you to the wedding, meeting my grandmother..." He shook his head hard, and his mouth twitched up in a smile for the first time since he'd reentered my room. "I never thought I'd be such a fool, but I guess I am. I am for you."

"You—" My voice broke. I was still shaking helplessly. "You love me?"

"Of course I love you." He frowned. "That's been pretty obvious for a while now, hasn't it?"

I stared at him speechlessly.

203

"You knew that, didn't you?" He was obviously serious. He looked confused, surprised, and strangely frozen. "I've been falling all over myself around you for two months now. And I've been... acting like a besotted boy. I brought you to meet my grandmother! Obviously, I love you. I thought you knew, and that's why you've been so careful around me and why you tried to let me down so gently just now."

I was almost choking on my surprise. And exhilaration. And joy.

It was definitely joy that was trapped in my throat.

"I didn't know!" I managed to rasp. "Damn it, Sean. I didn't know! I was being careful for *me*. Not for you!"

Sean blinked and clenched my hands hard. "Really?"

"Yes, really!" I was slammed with so many feelings at once that they had to come out some way. I pulled my hands out of his grip and hit him on the chest with both of my palms. "How the hell was I supposed to know when you always act so cool about everything?"

He blinked again, but I could see enlightenment dawning on his face.

So much else dawning too.

Coming to light, breaking into life, in the transformation of his expression.

"I always act cool," he said in a thick voice. "It doesn't mean anything. I thought you knew that."

"I knew you felt things beneath it, but I didn't know... I didn't know... you felt things for *me*."

"Of course for you," he murmured, his voice even rougher with emotion as he grabbed my hands again and held them tight. "Especially for you." He swallowed visibly. "So does this mean you... you feel things for me?"

"Yes, I feel things for you."

"What things?" His eyes were searching, urgent, fierce with barely contained excitement.

"Lots of things." I felt ridiculously shy, ridiculously scared, which made no sense after what he'd just admitted to me. So I pushed away my hesitation and said, "I love you too. That's why I had to end it. If you weren't going to love me, then I couldn't—"

I wasn't able to finish my sentence because Sean had pushed himself up off his knees and grabbed my head to kiss me.

I didn't mind at all. Whatever I was going to add to my confession just wasn't essential at the moment.

What was essential was Sean's lips against mine, his body pushing me down onto the bed, his heat and his weight and his urgency and the deep feeling I could feel coming off him in waves.

"You love me, Ash?" he murmured against my lips.

My hands were clenched in his hair, and my legs had wound around his hips. "Yes. I love you."

He groaned and kissed me again. Then he kept kissing me as he mumbled, "I love you, I love you, I love you, baby. I love you so much. I can't believe you didn't know."

The last bit caused me to break the kiss and give him a little glare. "Don't try to put this on me. You're the one who hid how he felt."

His eyes were laughing and caressing me at exactly the same time. "And you didn't?"

"I might have too. Just a little bit."

He chuckled and kissed me again, and he didn't stop for a long time.

Eventually the kissing deepened to fondling and then to taking off our clothes. When he was buried inside me, my legs bent up toward my chest and hands holding on to his neck, when we were rocking together in a fast, needy motion, he was still trying to kiss me, still muttering about how much he loved me, needed me, never wanted to let me go.

I might have been mumbling stuff back to him. I don't really know. I do know I was halfway crying, and there was no way to make myself stop.

I came anyway, gasping his name, and then he came too, choking on a helpless exclamation that sounded a lot like love.

He collapsed on me afterward, pressing little kisses against my mouth, my skin, my throat.

I stroked his back, my whole body sated in a way that was emotional as much as physical.

I could tell the difference.

I never wanted to have sex with anyone again when it didn't feel like this.

"When did you know that you loved me?" I asked after a few minutes of lying tangled up with him. We hadn't used a condom since we'd both been too carried away, but I was on birth control and I wasn't concerned.

Sean lifted his head, and I still couldn't believe the look in his eyes—completely unguarded, so deep.

So warm and soft and fond.

"I don't know," he admitted. "It grew slowly, but I guess it really hit me after you told me you'd had drinks with the jackass before you came to see me. Damn, I was torn up about that."

"You didn't act torn up. You acted…"

"Like an ass. I know." He gave me his quirk of a smile. "Why do you think that was?"

206

I giggled and slid my hands down his back to his butt. I squeezed there, foolishly thrilled that I was allowed to do so. "I didn't know."

"And when did you know you loved me?" he asked.

"I've been pretending not to for a long time," I admitted. "Pretending to myself. I didn't admit it until I broke up with you just a little while ago."

"You're a better person than I am. I would have gone on desperately in love with you and too scared to say anything for who knows how long, had you not pressed the issue."

I leaned up to kiss him. "Well, we figured it out then."

"Yes, we figured it out."

~

We stayed in bed for most of the day, getting up only occasionally to use the bathroom or to eat something.

We weren't making love constantly, of course. We were talking or resting or smiling at each other like sappy fools.

I don't remember ever having a better day, and I could tell Sean felt the same way.

We did have sex a few times, mostly soft and sweet although at one point we really got going, and he had me on my knees, bent over and clinging to the headboard, my body jiggling wildly as he took me from behind and made me come over and over again.

We were both exhausted after that and took a two-hour nap.

At about four the following morning, Sean finally got up to leave. He had to be at work by eight that morning, and so did I.

The world didn't come to a halt just because you found love. Life and work and schedules happened just the same.

I walked him to the front door of my apartment, and he gave me a soft kiss before he turned the doorknob. "Are you free this evening?" he asked with a smile.

"Yes. Monday nights aren't usually very busy for me. Did you want to meet at the hotel?"

"No." He was frowning at me now. "I wanted to take you to dinner. We've never actually had a date, you know."

I stared at him for a moment, my heart bursting with a new explosion of joy. "I guess we haven't. I'd love to have dinner with you."

"Good. I'll call you later." He kissed me again and then gently stroked a hand down my tangled hair. It wasn't looking good after so much sex and so many hours in bed. "You still love me?"

I laughed and reached up to cup his cheek with one hand. "I love you even more now."

"Good. Me too."

~

We did have dinner that Monday night. And at the end of the evening we tore up our contract together.

We had dinner on a lot of nights that followed.

We didn't have any of the normal, casual dating period, when you see the person once or twice a week and hesitate about when or how often to call them. All our preliminaries happened on those Wednesday nights in the hotel. I saw Sean almost every day, and on the few days we were too busy, he called me.

After about three weeks, I was regularly spending the night at his apartment since it was so much easier than to go back and forth to mine after I'd spent the evenings with him. Sean lived downtown, near where both of us worked. His place was much nicer than mine, and it saved me an annoying commute.

Plus I kind of liked sleeping with him.

All right. There was no "kind of" about it. I definitely liked sleeping with him. And waking up with him.

And doing a lot of other things with him too.

About a month after my sister's wedding, on a Saturday evening, we were coming into Sean's apartment together at about ten o'clock at night. And I was thinking that it felt like coming home.

Coming home.

Into Sean Doyle's apartment.

Six months ago, I'd never have even dreamed such a thing was possible.

I put my purse on the entryway table where I always left it and stared down at it for a minute, feeling strange, surreal.

Sean was already toeing off his shoes. He was dressed casually today in jeans and a gray long-sleeve, crewneck shirt. For so long in our relationship, I'd never seen him dressed that way. Only in suits. Or in a pair of his sleep pants.

Or naked.

But right now he was wearing jeans.

He frowned at me. "What's the matter?"

"Nothing."

His frown deepened as he came over to where I still stood by my purse. "Why are you lying to me?"

I rolled my eyes. "I wasn't really lying. It's just one of those things people say."

He put his hands on my shoulders and turned me around to face him. "I don't care if it's what people say. You said nothing is bothering you when I can clearly see it is."

One thing about being in a relationship with Sean was that I was never able to brush something off if he wanted to know it. If he got something between his teeth, he never let it go. Occasionally that got annoying, but I wasn't annoyed tonight. I shook my head. "Honestly, I was just standing here thinking how strange it is that it... it feels normal, coming into your place like this. Like I..."

"Belong here?" he murmured.

"Yeah."

"You do. What's strange about that?"

"Well, you're Sean Doyle. And this place is like a palace next to my little apartment."

"I like your place." He clearly meant it. Despite his money, he was never ostentatious about his possessions. As far as I could tell, he didn't buy things just to prove that he could. He wasn't insecure like that. Or a show-off.

"I know. I like it too. I just meant that I'm a normal girl."

His mouth turned downward again. "Are you saying I'm not a normal guy? Surely you can see that I am since we just spent hours with my family."

Right. There was that. I'd just spent the afternoon at a cookout with his parents, his brothers, his sister and her family, and his grandmother. It was the first family event I'd accompanied Sean too. It felt pretty significant.

Maybe that was why I was feeling so surreal now, as if my new reality was finally catching up with me.

"Ash?" Sean asked softly.

I blinked, thinking back to what he'd actually said. "Oh. No, I wasn't saying you're not normal. I'm just saying... it's different. Feeling at home in a place like this. I never expected to feel this way."

"Desperately in love with me?" Sean quirked up his lip.

I laughed and pulled him into a hug. "Yes. Exactly. I never expected to fall in love with you—or anything that's come with it."

He hugged me back, more tightly than I was expecting, so when I finally pulled away, I looked closely at his face. He always had a lot going on inside him, under the clever, charming demeanor he wore, and he didn't always tell me what it was unless I asked.

I watched him as we went into the living room and he collapsed on the leather couch, putting his feet up and stretching out to get comfortable and checking something on his phone.

I moved his feet so I could sit down and then put his feet in my lap.

"What were you worried about?" I asked after Sean lowered his phone.

"When?"

"Just now. By the door. When you asked me what was wrong. What were you worried about?"

I could see enlightenment flicker across the face, so I knew he understood what I was referring to. He opened his mouth. Closed it again. Then said, "You were kind of quiet on the way home. Then you looked like something had hit home with you. I thought..." He gave an ironic huff of amusement. "I thought maybe the family thing had been too much."

I rolled my eyes. "It was fine. I told you it was. They were all nice to me, and you know I love your grandmother."

"I know you do," he murmured with a fond expression that only lasted a few seconds. "But still… that's what I was worried about. That you were feeling… pressure."

I just looked at him, wondering if he could still be doubting my feelings for him—even after our being together like this for a month.

"It's not that I doubt you love me," he went on, as if he had read my mind. "But it's different. Being together in that hotel room. Being together here. Being just us. It's different than being thrown into the middle of a big family."

I nodded since he was right. "It is different," I admitted. "It's different. Living life with you. It's different from that hotel room. It's different and it's harder and it's scarier and it's better. It's *better*, Sean."

He smiled—just a tiny little lift of his mobile mouth. "I think so too."

I absently rubbed his feet, which were still in my lap. As far as men's feet go, his were pretty nice, and he still had his socks on.

I worked on his feet for a while, and I could feel the muscles in his legs relaxing. He exhaled loudly a few times, as if he liked how it felt.

When I glanced over at his face, his eyes were closed, and I felt the most ridiculous surge of affection for him, as if I could just swallow him whole.

He opened his eyes just then and might have caught the sappy look on my face.

His smile was just a little smug.

The only appropriate response to that expression was to change my sappy look to a cool glare.

He chuckled and sat up to reach for me. With a little rearranging, I was stretched out on the couch with him, my body pressed against his, one of his arms wrapped around me.

"So what did you really think of my family?" he asked.

I let out a breath and played with the fabric of his shirt. I liked how it felt. I liked that it was his. "They were nice."

"And?"

"They didn't ask me a bunch of nosy questions or anything, which was a relief."

"And?"

"They seem like they're happy that you're happy."

"And?"

I paused for a minute, clenching my hand in his shirt. Then I told him the truth. "I don't like that you're not included on that wall of photos."

There had been a wall in the living room of his parents' house that displayed framed photos of so many of the family members in their police uniforms. Sean wasn't included. He wasn't a cop.

"That's only for—"

"I know. I know. I still don't like it."

He brushed a kiss into my hair. "They love me."

"I know they do. I could tell. But I'd have thought…" I trailed off.

"You'd have thought what?"

"I'd have thought they would have been prouder of you."

"I made a lot of money. That's not the same, you know."

I adjusted so I could lift my head and look down at his face. "It's not just your money. It's everything you've done. It's

213

who you are. You deserve to be on the wall of honor. You're so amazing, Sean. *I'm* proud of you."

"You are?" His voice was soft and thick, and his face was full of emotion that reflected how I'd been feeling about him just a few minutes before. That almost embarrassing overflow of sappy emotion.

"Yes."

He pulled my head down so he could kiss me. "I'm proud of you too."

"For what?"

"For everything."

He settled against me again. He seemed tired this evening, and so was I. I didn't really feel like having sex. I just wanted to lie with him like this.

That was what we did. We fell asleep together on the couch.

~

A few weeks after that, we went to a play at the same theater where we'd run into each other at the ballet, on my one and only real date with John.

This time I was the one in the box with Sean. I had to admit that I liked it.

I could have done without all the curious stares, but I was getting used to it. Whoever was with Sean was going to get noticed. I wasn't the kind of person who liked to be the center of attention, but it was a minor inconvenience in the scheme of things.

The play was good, and we both enjoyed it. Sean seemed like he was in a good mood all evening, which was why

I was surprised at his reaction to my suggestion that we walk down the block to a cupcake shop afterward.

He agreed, but he didn't seem happy about it.

"We don't have to," I said, trying to figure out what had happened in the past two minutes to cause his change in attitude. He looked stiff and guarded, and I had no idea why. "If you're tired, we can—"

"I'm not tired. I said it was fine."

He might have said it was fine, but he clearly didn't mean it. He took my hand as we left the theater, and he didn't say a word as we started to walk down the sidewalk, which was crowded from everyone leaving the theater.

I peered at Sean's face in the bright streetlights as we walked. He looked as sexy and sophisticated as ever in his expensive suit and five-o'clock shadow, but something was definitely wrong. He was tense. His lips were pressed together. He stared straight ahead of us, and his hand was gripping mine so tightly it actually hurt.

"Sean?" I asked, bewildered and worried.

He took a deep breath and looked over at me slowly. Then he jerked visibly when someone shouted farther down the block. It sounded just like a brief, random argument between two men, but Sean sucked in a breath and pulled me against him protectively.

And I suddenly realized what was wrong.

I'd been an absolute idiot not to know from the beginning.

"Oh my God, Sean. I'm so sorry." I reached up to take his face in my hands. He was paler than he should have been and incredibly tense. "I wasn't thinking. I'm so, so sorry."

He'd been shot less than three years ago on a city sidewalk a lot like this one, walking home from the theater.

Lara had been killed.

He'd told me about that night a few times in the past month or two. How the police had concluded it was a random crime, a mugging gone wrong since no further attempt on Sean's life had followed the incident. He'd even hired a bodyguard for a few months after he got out of the hospital, but he hadn't liked living that way. No one had been trying to kill him anyway.

It had been a thoughtless, meaningless tragedy, as so many heartbreaks are.

And like an idiot, I hadn't even thought that making him do the same thing now might bring back to him that terrible night.

"It's okay, Ash," he said, his voice rough with suppressed emotion. "It's not a big deal."

"It *is* a big deal." I was so upset that tears were streaming down my face. "I can't believe I didn't even think about it. I'm so sorry."

My tears seemed to have an effect on him. His face twisted briefly, and he wiped away the tears with his thumbs. "Please don't cry, baby. You didn't do anything wrong."

"Yes, I did."

"No, you didn't. This is just one of those... those leftovers. I think I'm basically over it. Not that I'll forget about Lara, but I really think I've healed. And I'm so happy now with you. But then we walked outside here, and I kept imagining something happening to you, and I..." He shook his head and took a ragged breath.

"I never should have suggested we do this. Let's go back to the car and go home." I grabbed the lapels of his suit jacket and turned him toward where the car and driver he'd hired was waiting down the block.

Sean wouldn't move. "You wanted a cupcake."

"I don't need a cupcake. Seriously, Sean. There's no reason you have to do this."

"I want to." His face was getting its color back, and he'd squared his shoulders. "I know I don't have to, but I want to. This isn't PTSD or something like that. I'm just... I'm just scared. It was random. The chances of it happening again are almost zero. I don't want to always be scared."

"You don't have to push through this, Sean." I was still holding on to his jacket.

"I want to."

I nodded silently and took his arm. If he wanted to do this, then I would do it with him.

I was still crying a little as we walked, but I didn't let go of his arm, even to wipe my face. Sean didn't say anything, but his expression and his posture seemed to relax after he'd taken a few steps, as if the conversation and his act of will had pushed him over the worst of the fear.

We reached the cupcake shop, and nothing happened.

He opened the door for me.

We walked in.

We got in the long line at the counter.

Sean reached out to take my hand in his.

With a strangled exclamation, I wrapped my arms around him and buried my face in his chest.

Sean hugged me back.

After a minute, he murmured into my ear, "Uh, baby?"

I made a sound in response, but it was muffled by his jacket.

"I thought I was the one about to have a breakdown."

I half sobbed and half giggled as I finally lifted my face to smile up at him. "I was having the breakdown for both of us. That's okay, isn't it?"

Sean's expression cracked slightly, and he grabbed me in another tight hug.

He didn't say anything, but he didn't have to.

We'd been together for real for going on two months, and I'd known from that morning we got together, after my sister's wedding, that both our feelings were real, were lasting.

I'd known Sean was the love of my life so much better than my romantic daydreams, so much better than my second best.

But sometimes you know even more than that.

Sometimes living in love with someone else reveals truths about the world—truths you never knew before.

Maybe it was an obvious conclusion, something I should have known all along.

But there's knowing something and there's really understanding it.

What I had with Sean wouldn't just make my life happier. It would also make my life harder.

Loving someone else always does.

That's what makes it so good.

We held on to each other until we reached the counter.

Then we ordered our cupcakes.

EPILOGUE

Five months later, on a Wednesday evening, I left work and walked down the block to a familiar hotel.

I hadn't stepped through those doors into the lobby for months now, but Sean had texted me at lunchtime and asked if I'd come over after work.

I knew why.

I might pretend not to be sentimental, but I am.

Today was exactly one year from that first evening we spent together.

On a Wednesday night.

In this hotel.

It was very sweet that he'd remembered.

The elevator smelled exactly as it always had—that faint combination of expensive aftershave and cleaning products. If the scent had been strong, it would have been unpleasant, but it was just barely there.

I kind of liked it.

It evoked all kinds of powerful memories.

I leaned against the wall of the elevator as it ascended, closing my eyes as I waited. I was actually quite tired this evening. For the past three weeks, I'd been working on a big project. It was a good thing—a definite step up for my career—but I'd had to put in long hours and had stayed awake at night thinking about it.

I hoped Sean didn't have plans for some sort of sex marathon tonight.

I wasn't sure I was up for it.

When the elevator made it to the twelfth floor, I stepped off and walked down the hall, pausing in front of the mirror. Today, I wore a dark green skirt suit and a new pair of heels. My hair was as straight and un-tousle-able as ever.

Love unfortunately didn't cause one's hair to turn miraculously sexy.

Shaking my head at my reflection, I continued to the door for room 1212.

I knocked.

After a few seconds, the door swung open, and Sean looked at me over the threshold with an arch of one eyebrow and a little twitch of his mouth. He wore nothing but a pair of soft black sleep pants, and his hair was a bit damp at the edges. He'd obviously just gotten out of the shower.

"Are you trying to be sexy?" I asked him.

He frowned. "Trying?"

I laughed and stepped forward to kiss him as he pushed the door closed.

He smelled clean and delicious, and his body was warm and hard. He walked me backward into the room as his mouth moved against mine, pulling the strap of my bag off my shoulder and dropping it on the floor as we went.

"I guess you were anticipating in the shower," I mumbled as he eased me down onto the bed and moved over me. I was vaguely conscious of the bottle of red wine with two glasses on the table and a white bakery box on a side table, but the only thing I could focus on was Sean.

"I've been anticipating all afternoon." His shoulders and biceps were tense, but his smile was almost tender as he gazed down on me. His eyebrows drew together slightly. "You look tired."

"Thanks a lot." I pulled him down into another kiss so we wouldn't lose any momentum. "I've been anticipating too."

My kiss must have convinced him that I was sufficiently in the mood for sex because he immediately got going. He took off my clothes piece by piece, kissing and caressing the skin he revealed.

Tired or not, good sex is good sex. By the time he'd stripped me naked, I was very turned on. As he kissed his way down my bare belly, I was squirming beneath him and tugging eagerly at his hair.

His mouth continued its descent until he was nuzzling between my legs. I gasped and parted my thighs to make room for him. He pleasured me with his mouth until I couldn't hold still. My back was arching up off the bed, and I was clutching at my knees to hold my legs apart.

I bit my bottom lip in an attempt to quiet myself down, but it didn't really work.

Sean was way too good at this, and he was clearly stretching it out on purpose to extend my pleasure, to make me come even harder.

He was smiling when my orgasm finally broke and I completely lost control. He always liked it when I was loud.

As I sprawled out on the bed, flushed and wheezing, he was still smiling as he moved up my body.

"There's no reason for you to be smirking that way," I told him breathlessly.

"Really?" His green eyes caressed my damp face and naked body with such obvious fondness that my heart melted. Just a little. "You seemed to like what I did to you."

"I did," I told him, hooking my hands around his neck. "But that's irrelevant."

"Irrelevant?"

"Yes. Smirking will always be obnoxious."

He chuckled and kissed me. As he did, he rocked his hips against my middle. He was fully erect, and I loved how he felt pressed up against me—palpable proof of his desire, his need for me.

I knew from the tension in his body that he wasn't going to be able to hold out much longer, so I wasn't surprised when less than a minute had passed and he was pulling his erection out of his waistband and positioning himself at my entrance.

He bent my knees up toward my chest as he entered me, and then he started to thrust.

I was tight after my first orgasm, and the penetration was full and pleasurable. I gave a little whimper each time he pushed into me, and it matched the rough grunts he was making.

Our eyes met as we moved urgently together, and I couldn't look away. There was so much more than lust in Sean's eyes.

There was need and knowledge and affection and trust and memory and understanding.

It was love.

It was everything I'd ever known about love, and in all these months it had never wavered.

I knew it never would.

Sean wasn't going to last very long, but I didn't need him to. His fast, hard motion pushed me over the edge, and I came with a strangled sob just before he let go himself. We shook and gasped together until our bodies had relaxed.

Then we lay tangled up in a sated heap, enjoying the aftermath.

Sean occasionally pressed a little kiss into my neck.

After several minutes, he finally pushed himself up, which was good because his weight was starting to get uncomfortable. He held himself up above me on straightened arms and smiled. "You hungry?"

"God, yes."

"You want a steak?"

"What else?"

Just for the record, I didn't eat steak every night. But for our one-year anniversary of our first meeting here in the hotel, what else would I have ordered?

I went to the bathroom, took a quick shower, and changed into the pajamas I'd brought. Then we lay snuggled up on the bed until room service arrived with our food.

After we ate and split most of a bottle of wine, I felt perfectly sated, and I had no complaints in the world. I collapsed onto the bed and smiled up at the ceiling.

Sean was chuckling as he lowered himself beside me. "You look like you feel pretty good."

"I do." I turned my head to meet his gaze. "This was a really good idea. I can't believe it's only been a year since our first night together here. It feels like..."

"A lifetime."

That was exactly how I felt too—like we'd always been together. I found the energy to lean over and press my lips against his mouth. "I love you, Sean Doyle."

"And I love you too. More than anything."

"But don't think for a minute that this overflow of sappiness has made me fail to notice that box over on that table. You went to the bakery, didn't you?"

He laughed softly and reached out to brush my hair back off my face. "Is that what you think?"

"Yes, that's what I think. And I'm going to be digging into those cupcakes pretty soon, just so you know."

His eyes looked oddly excited, but his face was perfectly composed, with only one corner of his mouth twitching up. "It's not cupcakes."

My lips parted slightly. The truth was, I might have been a little disappointed by this piece of news. "What did you get then?"

"You better go and find out."

With a groan, I rolled off the bed. "This better be good since it required my standing up."

I took a few steps over to the side table where the bakery box was sitting.

I reached down to open the lid.

I tucked my hair behind my ear since it was blocking my view.

I looked inside the box.

I froze.

"What—" I couldn't get my voice to work any more than that.

Inside the box was a miniature wedding cake, beautifully iced and perfectly crafted in four tiny layers.

There was no other way to describe what I was seeing.

It was a wedding cake.

I stared for what felt like forever before I was finally able to blink.

Then I turned around to find Sean standing right behind me, holding out a beautifully engraved platinum ring with a diamond solitaire.

"Will you marry me, Ash?" he asked.

I was still frozen, surprise and joy and so much more crashing together inside me.

When I didn't answer, didn't even move, Sean's expression changed slightly. His brows drew together. "No?"

"Yes!" I threw myself into his arms and almost knocked him over.

My answer much have reassured him because he started to smile again and didn't really stop smiling for the rest of the evening.

I didn't either.

We ate the little wedding cake, which was delicious. We took a lot of breaks to admire the engagement ring on my finger, and we made sure to save a little piece for Sean to give to his grandmother.

Then we ended up back in bed.

We didn't make love again that night. I was too tired and giggly, and Sean was too happy to care.

It was the best night of my life. No contenders.

I'd had a lot of other really good nights with Sean over the past year. So many more that I would always remember. And so many more to come.

But that first night we met in the hotel, exactly a year ago, when Sean was still mostly a stranger to me. That night had opened up all the rest of them for us.

So that night was the second best.

ABOUT NOELLE ADAMS

Noelle handwrote her first romance novel in a spiral-bound notebook when she was twelve, and she hasn't stopped writing since. She has lived in eight different states and currently resides in Virginia, where she writes full time, reads any book she can get her hands on, and offers tribute to a very spoiled cocker spaniel.

She loves travel, art, history, and ice cream. After spending far too many years of her life in graduate school, she has decided to reorient her priorities and focus on writing contemporary romances. For more information, please check out her website: noelle-adams.com.

Books by Noelle Adams

Tea for Two Series
> Falling for her Brother's Best Friend
> Winning her Brother's Best Friend
> Seducing her Brother's Best Friend

Balm in Gilead Series
> Relinquish
> Surrender
> Retreat

Rothman Royals Series
> A Princess Next Door
> A Princess for a Bride

A Princess in Waiting
Christmas with a Prince

Preston's Mill Series (co-written with Samantha Chase)
Roommating
Speed Dating
Procreating

Eden Manor Series
One Week with her Rival
One Week with her (Ex) Stepbrother
One Week with her Husband
Christmas at Eden Manor

Beaufort Brides Series
Hired Bride
Substitute Bride
Accidental Bride

Heirs of Damon Series
Seducing the Enemy
Playing the Playboy
Engaging the Boss
Stripping the Billionaire

Willow Park Series
Married for Christmas
A Baby for Easter
A Family for Christmas
Reconciled for Easter
Home for Christmas

One Night Novellas

One Night with her Best Friend
One Night in the Ice Storm
One Night with her Bodyguard
One Night with her Boss
One Night with her Roommate
One Night with the Best Man

The Protectors Series (co-written with Samantha Chase)

Duty Bound
Honor Bound
Forever Bound
Home Bound

Standalones

A Negotiated Marriage
Listed
Bittersweet
Missing
Revival
Holiday Heat
Salvation
Excavated
Overexposed
Road Tripping
Chasing Jane
Late Fall
Fooling Around
Married by Contract
Trophy Wife

Bay Song
Her Reluctant Billionaire
Second Best

81190747R00140

Made in the USA
Columbia, SC
27 November 2017